COLD-BLOODED
GUN LAW

"Drop it," the sheriff ordered. "Walk over to the rail and drop it in the yard."

Cal stepped to the porch rail, reaching over it, but hesitating to drop a cocked and loaded rifle. Frisco Hays was standing in the yard below him and a little behind him near the porch. Sid Lun was at the other end of the porch near the steps. Hays seemed startled by the appearance of a rifle above him; he lunged to the corner of the porch as if to take cover ... Luna peeled his gun from its holster and fired twice fanning the hammer. Cal staggered ... gave the world a look of bewilderment, and collapsed ...

SHORTCUT TO DEVIL'S CLAW
The New Action Western
By WILLIAM O. TURNER

Shortcut to Devil's Claw

William O. Turner

A BERKLEY MEDALLION BOOK
published by
BERKLEY PUBLISHING CORPORATION

Harold Matson Company
22 East 40th Street
New York, N.Y. 10016

SBN 425-03410-2

BERKLEY MEDALLION BOOKS are published by
Berkley Publishing Corporation
200 Madison Avenue
New York, N.Y. 10016

BERKLEY MEDALLION BOOK ® TM 757,375

Printed in the United States of America

Berkley Medallion Edition, JUNE, 1977

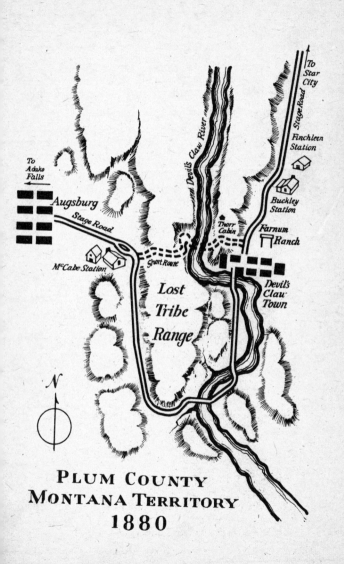

PLUM COUNTY
MONTANA TERRITORY
1880

1

IT WAS EASY enough. Eight haystacks, eight matches. That, plus a little hard riding in between to get them all ablaze quickly, was all it took.

It was less easy afterward for Jim Farnum to sit his horse a quarter mile away and watch Ike McCabe's hopes for a good year burn away in the night. He watched the shadow figures of the family as they moved in and out of the glow of the stack nearest the stage station. McCabe, his wife, his leggy kids. They were trying to save that one stack. It was the last he had touched off, and they'd been wakened by its leaping light. They'd formed a bucket line from the pump in the station yard. The effort was panicky, futile. You might as well spit on hell, Jim Farnum thought.

He spat into the darkness as if to rid himself of the taste of shame. Peavey & Company was the enemy, not McCabe. Peavey was a network of stage lines that sprawled north from the railroad over Idaho and half of Montana. McCabe ran a relay station for Peavey, so McCabe got hit. It was as simple and as unfair as that. This was the way you fought a stage war. Peavey had made the rules.

Jim Farnum's line was a much smaller operation, a hundred-and-ninety-mile, three-day run between Adako Falls and Devil's Claw. Jim had started it when he learned that there was a mail contract available, a contract that no one else, including Peavey & Company, was interested in at the time. Part of the route was a pack trail that you couldn't get an ox cart over, let alone a stagecoach. Jim had gone in with a road crew, and they'd graded and widened and built bridges. He'd set up relay stations, and he was in business.

For a few years there was no competition. Then mining towns sprang up north of Devil's Claw. Peavey & Company sent out a tentacle to them, following the Farnum route to Devil's Claw. It had put new Concord coaches on the run. It had cut fares. It had enticed Jim's best drivers away from him. But he had one vital advantage. He had the mail contract, and it kept him in the black.

Peavey had tried to buy him out, making a pathetic offer that barely covered the value of Jim's livestock. Jim turned it down politely. Peavey responded by hiring the notorious Jack Thorr, an old Overland troubleshooter who had become a railroad cop in the steel-laying days. He had tamed the boom towns and the rag camps, leaving dead men behind. He had been too ruthless even for the U. P., which had fired him. Now he was division superintendent for Peavey, and the war got dirty.

In some instances, Peavey had shared Farnum's relay stations. The arrangement was welcomed by stationkeepers, and Jim had made no objection. Then Thorr took over these stations exclusively, bullying and buying the keepers into refusing to board Farnum horses or feed Farnum passengers. Jim had set up new stations, hastily built cabins and corrals that served the purpose for the time being.

That was only the beginning. Jim's big barn at Augsburg burned to the ground, clearly the result of arson. Farnum coaches were sabotaged, delaying departures and causing breakdowns on the road. Stations were hit by raiders who ran off horses and scattered them in the mountains. Then, yesterday morning, a dozen horses were missing from Jim's Devil's Claw ranch. He found them in a box canyon, all shot dead.

The McCabe family had given up its attempt to save the haystack now. They had backed off from its heat and were staring out over their quarter section, probably counting the red holes in the night that were their other stacks. McCabe would have to haul a lot of hay this winter. And pay for it. He had just proved up on his homestead last month. Probably he'd have to take out a mortgage — if he didn't already have one.

Jim reined toward the stage road, making a wide circle around the station. I'm finally hitting back, he thought. The bastards will know they've pushed too hard. He tried to find a lift for his spirit in the thought, but there was none. Thorr would react quickly and viciously. The war would get meaner, more dangerous. The law would be of no help. Peavey & Company owned lawyers as other men owned horses. And it owned the sheriff of Plum County.

I'll lose, Jim thought. I ought to quit. I ought to drive my horses to the railroad and get some kind of price for them. And the coaches and the harness, they'd bring a few dollars, too. I'd keep the ranch, settle down on it, raise horses. But not now, not yet. Not till I've put up a fight Peavey and Thorr won't forget.

He followed the road for a short distance; then he headed straight into the mountains to his left. This was the Lost Tribe range, a high ragged wall with the stage road winding southeastward along its base. Eventually, after thirty miles, the road rolled over a saddle in the range and slanted back northward on the other side of it to Devil's Claw town.

There was no other way over the Lost Tribes, it was believed, not even a trail. Even the oldtimers believed that, even the prospectors and the surveyors and the goat hunters. Oh, a climber might make it, with ropes and such. But there was no way a man could walk over, let

3

alone cross on horseback. Anyone who lived in this country would tell you that and would regard you as a greenhorn for asking.

But it was not true, and Jim Farnum knew it was not.

Back in the days when he and his crew were transforming the roundabout pack trail into a road, an old mountain man had joined them. He was very old and a little crazy, haunted by the time when beaver had been plentiful and civilization far away. When the crew had moved up the east side of the range to Devil's Claw, the old man had stolen four horses and headed straight into the mountains. Jim had gone after him, thinking him trapped. The trail led up the Devil's Claw river into a high-walled gorge that paralleled the chine of the range. The stream filled the gorge from wall to wall. Jim had spent a day figuring out where the mountain man had gone. By the time he got the answer the old duffer was over the crest of the Lost Tribes and out of them and gone forever. But Jim had learned that there was a way over the range.

He trusted no one with his secret except his wife, simply because the passage was much too convenient for horse thieves. He had staked out a ranch just north of Devil's Claw town and had stocked it with horses that were being broken and trained for his coaches. He had chosen the site with an eye to security; there had seemed to be no way out of the long rolling valley except straight north or straight south. Now there was this new way to the west, and to reveal its existence might have been costly.

Now there was another reason that Jim Farnum was glad he had kept his secret. This mountain shortcut would provide him with his alibi.

The town of Devil's Claw was a bit more than sixty miles from McCabe station by the mountain-circling stage road — an all-night ride even if you changed horses along the way. The route up and over the range was scarcely more than twenty miles. Some of them were steep miles, but a good horse could cover the distance easily in four hours. To copper his bet, Jim had a relief mount picketed in a little ravine this side of the summit.

He'd made it a point to be seen by several people in Devil's Claw last evening. He would be on hand again before six this morning to see his westbound coach hitched and loaded. No one would consider it possible that he had made a round trip to McCabe station in the interval.

He traveled steadily in the darkness, but carefully. The way over the range was not so rugged as a man might expect. There were no shale-slippery ledges to cross, no long, horse-killing grades. But there was no well-defined trail, either. There was just a way over the mountains if you made the right turns. The danger was that he would miss a landmark and get lost.

Just before dawn, wet from the river crossing, he rode down the last long slope and reached the stage road again. He was north of Devil's Claw and almost at the gate of his ranch. He swung south along the road, passing the ranch, and then cut cross-country to the outskirts of the sleeping town.

His house was on a knoll overlooking the little settlement that sprawled out raggedly from the core of its business street. He stabled his two horses in a shed and entered the house by the back door. He went through the dark kitchen and the hall to the bedroom and found a lamp burning and April sitting up in bed. There was a slender book in her hands, and he wondered if she had slept at all.

She closed the book and laid it aside. "You did it?"

Poetry, he thought. She was a rare woman, a reminder that there was more to a life than work and strife and money.

5

"Yes."

There were no secrets between them, no lies, but he wished she hadn't had to know where he had been last night and what he had done. Technically, he supposed, she was an accomplice.

"I'll make coffee," she said.

"Not for me. I'll get breakfast at the Greek's."

She nodded, hugging her knees, understanding that he wanted to be seen early and by as many people as possible. She sighed sharply. "What good's it going to do, Jim?"

"I'm fighting back."

"And they'll fight back, and you'll fight back, and it will go on until you're destroyed."

"If I can make the fight costly enough for Peavey, he'll make a new offer, better than the last."

"You'll take it?"

"It's the only chance I have."

He shaved, changed clothes and walked to the Farnum barn to see the coach readied for the three-day run to Adako Falls. He rode the two blocks to the hotel beside the driver. He helped load mail and baggage, chatting with the postmaster and with Bud Beasely, the deputy sheriff stationed here. When the coach had left, he went to breakfast at Constantine's OK Cafe, sitting at a table with the cashier of the bank and the town barber.

After that, he spent a couple of hours at his office, going over accounts with Link Arbuckle, his general manager. He went home then and slept until the middle of the afternoon. When he returned to the office, Link confronted him nervously.

"McCabe rode into town a little while ago, Jim."

Jim met Link's dark eyes and saw the concern in them. "So it's all over town by now."

"My God, Jim!"

"Beasely will be around with questions, I suppose."

"McCabe went to Augsburg first. The sheriff sent him here to alert Beasely. They'll bear down on this, Jim."

Link was a big, angular man in his thirties, easy-going and likable. He had been a driver and had ridden shotgun on occasion, but he was a man who disliked violence.

"They'll get whoever you hired to burn the hay," he said. "He'll name the man who hired him. They'll beat it out of him."

"I didn't hire anybody, Link."

"You went through a third party?"

"The less you know, the better."

"I guess so." Link sank into a chair.

"It's Thorr I'm worried about, not the law," Jim said. "You'd better get out to the ranch. Be sure the horses are in close and there's a tight watch on them. And send a couple of men into town to stay with Abe at the barn tonight. See that they have shotguns."

"You think he'll try for the barn?"

"The man is a little crazy," Jim said. "God knows what he'll try for."

Link got up, clamped a hat on wiry dark hair and went out. Jim sank into a chair and lighted a cigar. Ten minutes later, roly-poly Bud Beasely came in.

Bud wore his deputy's badge pinned to his hat. He took off the hat and studied the badge as if trying to see his reflection in it.

"Somebody burned McCabe's hay."

"I know," Jim said.

"You hired it done?"

"No."

"One of your people done it. You deny that?"

"Yes."

"Well, I got to ask these questions," Bud said. He was

7

young, inclined to chubbiness, and all starch and shine from boot tips to neatly waxed little oxbow mustache. "I won't get nothing out of you except the satisfaction of making you lie, I know that. Thorr had your horses shot. You had his hay burned."

"Thorr had my horses shot. Lightning struck his hay."

Bud put on his hat. "You shouldn't have done it, Farnum. If the law don't get you, Thorr will."

"Thorr and his hired toughs have played dirty for a long time. The law let them get away with it. Now maybe I'm going to hit back. Maybe the law has a war on its hands."

Beasely shook his head sadly. "You'll lose," he said as he left the office.

An hour later, Jim watched from the window as the Peavey northbound arrived, discharging a full load of passengers, some of whom would stay overnight at the hotel and go on to Star City in the morning. The Farnum coach pulled in a few minutes later. It carried only two women and a small boy.

Jim rode it to the barn and saw the team unhitched and stabled. Abe Klingerman, the stableman, was tense, edgy. So were the two ranch hands that Link had sent in as guards. Jim wanted to steady them and didn't quite know how.

"Don't shoot anybody you don't have to," he said, grinning and trying to make a joke of it.

The sun was setting when he got home. April had supper ready, corned beef and sauerkraut. It was one of his favorites, and he was hungry. They ate leisurely in the fragrant warmth of the kitchen, and they talked easily, not mentioning McCabe or Peavey & Company or Thorr.

They had lighted a lamp, and he was drying dishes for her when the men burst in, two through the back door, two coming in through the parlor. Their faces were covered

8

with bandannas with eye holes cut out of them. Two held revolvers, a third a shotgun. The fourth held a coiled bull whip. One of the men seized April by the hair and thrust a revolver in her face.

"Leave her alone," Jim said. "I'll give you no trouble."

"Take her into the bedroom," the man with the whip said. His voice was muffled by his mask, but Jim was sure he recognized it.

"If you touch her — "

"Tear up a sheet," the man with the whip said. "Tie her to the bed."

April was pulled out of the room. Jim took a step toward the man with the whip, shoving the man with the shotgun aside.

"Damn it, your quarrel is with me. If you — "

The man with the shotgun crashed its butt against Jim's skull. Jim didn't see the blow coming, and it caught him solidly. He took one reeling step and sprawled face down on the floor.

"Get him up," the man with the whip said. He shook out the whip and cracked it. "Lay him out on the table."

The other two men bent over Jim's limp body. They started to lift him, then put him down, turning him on his back.

"He's dead weight, Jack," one of them said. "He's cold. He ain't going to feel anything."

The other man felt Jim's wrist for a pulse. He shook his head, then he put an ear against Jim's chest.

"For Christ's sake," the man with the whip said. "He ain't dead. Get him on the table."

"I think he is, Jack. I truly think he is."

The whip snapped across the room, its copper tip slicing through Jim's shirt and into the flesh of his chest.

There was no reaction at all from Jim's body, no moan, no reflexive wrench, no twitch of muscles.

"For Christ's sake," the man with the whip said.

Forty minutes later, wrists raw from a struggle with her bonds, April staggered into the kitchen and knelt beside her husband. She said his name, lifted his head, felt the clamminess of his skin. A great cry filled the room, not a scream, but a sound such as she had never heard before and that she didn't think of as coming from herself.

Jim Farnum was indeed dead.

2

PUBLICLY, APRIL FARNUM reacted to her husband's death with a show of stoic acceptance. The people of Devil's Claw admired her for that. They said that she must have a deep inner faith in order to accept God's will so gracefully.

Privately, she didn't consider for a moment that Jim's murder was God's will. It was a fact, that was all, and eventually she did accept it. But not until she had gone through more kinds of hell than she ever let anybody know.

There were the first stunned twenty-four hours when nothing was real and there was only an agonizing emptiness. Link Arbuckle's widowed cousin, Sally Smithwick, stayed with her. Link was there a good deal of the time, too, making funeral arrangements, running errands, doing chores. April was grateful to both of them but took little comfort from their presence or from anything else.

She walked through the funeral without a tear, feeling little except a sense of unreality and a desire to get the formalities over with. Friends came to her house afterward, bringing pies and cakes and such. Sally Smithwick made tea. There were even little jokes and laughter, which come easily after a funeral. April smiled and chatted, emotions buried.

The next day Sheriff Haller, who had questioned her earlier, came over from Augsburg again. A certain amount of below-the-belt nastiness between competing stage lines was to be expected, he told her, but he, by God — pardon me, ma'am — wasn't going to tolerate the brutal murder of a man in his own home. The whole of Plum county was outraged and he damn well — pardon me, ma'am — was outraged, too.

"The trouble is you can't identify any of those men who busted in," he said. He paused, eyeing her closely. It seemed to her that he looked reassured when she shook her head. "I don't intend to let that stop me, ma'am. I'll find out who did it."

The truth was she did know who one of the men was. She was completely sure, but how could she say that when he had worn a mask? In any case, she saw nothing to be gained by telling a law officer who was on the Peavey payroll and would protect Peavey people. She managed a nod and a look of appreciation, but the word in her mind was "hypocrite." The sheriff gave a hitch to his gunbelt and strutted off like a self-conscious angel of justice girded for battle.

April began to sort herself out now, to put names to her feelings. The clearest and sharpest was anger, and for a while she fed its flame. She paced her room, sometimes talking to herself. She stared from her window down at the ragged housetops of the town and hated its complacency.

There was color in her cheeks that night when she sat down to the supper Sally had cooked. Link was there, too; Sally must have invited him. They remarked about the improvement in her appearance.

She slept little, feeding the flame again, nourishing it with violent thoughts and fantasies. She would sell the stage line, no matter for how little. Then, no longer vulnerable, she would burn Peavey barns, run off Peavey horses, rob Peavey stages. She would become a bandit queen, riding at the head of a gang that would ravish Peavey holdings over the whole territory. Her gunfighters would kill Jack Thorr. No, she would walk into his office with Jim's shotgun and personally blow him to Kingdom Come....

She slept a little before dawn. When she woke, the flame had burned down. She could think clearly and felt that she was herself at last. After breakfast she walked to the Farnum office and had a talk with Link.

"I'm going to run the Farnum line," she told him. "I'll take Jim's place. I'll have to rely on you very heavily, of course, especially at first."

Link nodded, frowning at the same time. "Peavey will make you an offer for the line soon, I expect."

"Have there been feelers?"

"Not exactly. But Jim's death was — well, it was sort of an accident, April. They meant to give him a whipping, not to kill him. But they did, and the sheriff is right about one thing. People are outraged. A lot of them are shunning Peavey's stages, and we've had a bigger share of the passenger traffic the last few days. They'll get over it soon enough, I suppose, but until they do, Peavey will have to stop the rough stuff. Yes, it's logical that there'll be an offer now."

"If you get a chance, hint that I might be interested."

Link ran a hand over his wiry dark hair. "Whatever you say."

"I won't sell for what they'll offer, but I want them to come to me. Meanwhile, I have a lot to learn about the details of running a stage line. I'll be on hand to see the coach off in the morning."

"You needn't get up that early. I can — "

"I know you can," she said. "But Jim did it, and I'm going to do it. Every morning."

"Whatever you say. But — I mean, do you think it's what Jim would want?"

"He'd want me to do what *I* want. I'm going to run this line, Link. And I warn you. I'm not necessarily going to run it the way Jim would."

13

Link showed mild surprise, then he grinned. "Okay, Boss."

The next few days were long and tiring for her. She saw the westbound load at six A.M., and she was on hand when the eastbound ended its three-day journey from Idaho at six-thirty in the evening. In the hours between she worked steadily in the office helping the clerk, selling tickets, registering express shipments, memorizing schedules, studying accounts. She sent to the land office at Helena for a large map of the county and, mysteriously, spent a lot of time studying that, too. When she had some elemental grasp of the details of the business, she slowed down a bit, taking a long noon hour as Jim had often done. Sometimes she even allowed herself the luxury of a brief nap after lunch.

Peavey & Company made its overture sooner than she expected. It came in the form of a letter from G.T. Peavey himself, announcing that he would be in Devil's Claw the following week and would like to discuss a business matter with her. She answered promptly, setting a time and suggesting that they meet at the Farnum office.

When the day came, she put on a rather formal gray suit with collar and cuffs trimmed in black velvet. She waited in the inner office with Tom Lawrence, her attorney. Tom was a graying man in a rumpled suit who smelled vaguely of whiskey. He was an outspoken believer in such causes as women's suffrage, more generous treatment of Indians, free love, squatters' rights and abolition of the bounty on coyotes. He was not a popular man, but in April's opinion he was an honest one.

Link met Peavey in the outer office and brought him in. He was accompanied by a lawyer, a chubby, well-barbered man named Sample. Jack Thorr was not with

14

them. His absence, April thought, was a tactful touch, and it was also an admission of guilt.

Gus Peavey was in his early sixties, a knobby-faced old bandit who looked uncomfortable in a winged collar and black bow tie. He carried a walking stick and an unlighted cigar. Tom Lawrence rose and shook hands as Link performed the introductions. April managed a smile and a nod but did not offer her hand. They all sat down.

"First of all, ma'am," Gus Peavey said, "please accept my sympathy and my regret for the tragic — "

"Spare me that, Mr. Peavey. Shall we get right down to business?"

Peavey waved this cigar in a little gesture of resignation. "I'm here in good faith, Mrs. Farnum, and I'll speak my mind. I'd like to put an end to the nastiness that has been going on — on both sides — and I've come to make an offer for your stage line. Mr. Sample has drawn up a tentative contract of sale, subject to negotiation in regard to details of course."

They were sitting at an oblong table that April had cleared for the occasion. Sample passed a folded document across to her. She held it suspended above the table, not unfolding it.

"How much are you offering?" she asked.

Peavey exchanged a look with Sample. "Seven thousand dollars."

"For the entire assets of the Farnum line?"

"Yes, ma'am," Sample said. "Naturally. Not including, however, your ranch or your home."

"But including the horses on the ranch?"

"The contract calls for two hundred horses," Sample said. "We assume that is approximately your total stock."

15

"I might point out," Peavey said, "that this offer is five hundred dollars more than the one I made to your husband."

"Two hundred horses," April said, "ten coaches, barns and other real estate, harness and miscellaneous equipment — seven thousand dollars is a paltry offer, Mr. Peavey."

Peavey had been chewing on his unlighted cigar. He took it from his mouth, its end in shreds. April looked at it with distaste.

"Let's call a spade a spade," Peavey said. "I don't need two hundred horses or ten coaches or any of the rest of it except the mail contract. Yes, I want that; but when it comes up for renewal, I'll outbid you and get it anyway."

"The contract has another three years to run," Tom Lawrence pointed out.

"Exactly. That's the only reason I'm making an offer at all."

"And three years from now, if you buy me out, you'll be the only bidder," April said. "You'll have things your own way."

Peavey nodded curtly and stuck the cigar back in his mouth. "A point for you, Mrs. Farnum."

"If all you want is the contract, how much will you offer for that alone? I can sell the horses and equipment elsewhere. To Gilmer and Salisbury probably."

Gilmer and Salisbury were one of the largest lines in the country and were getting larger. In several places they were in competition with Peavey and were getting the best of it.

"You can't sell the contract alone," Sample said. "It can be transferred only by selling your company."

"She can do that without selling coaches and live-stock," Tom Lawrence said quickly.

"That depends," Sample said.

"You lawyers shut up," Peavey said. "Mrs. Farnum, I'll up my price one thousand dollars. I'll pay you eight thousand for the whole shebang. I will not go one penny higher."

April still held the unfolded contract in one hand. She let it drop onto the table. "No."

Peavey took the cigar from his mouth and looked around uncomfortably. He considered a cuspidor that stood in a corner some eight feet away, then changed his mind.

"Forgive me, Mrs. Farnum," Sample said, "but staging is a hard business. Surely you'd like to get out of it. Eight thousand dollars is a lot of money."

"You're wrong, Mr. Sample. I don't particularly want to get out of it."

Link Arbuckle spoke for the first time. "If you divide two hundred horses into eight thousand dollars, leaving the coaches and the mail contract out of it, you get forty dollars a horse. That's a cow-pony price. A good coach horse is worth twice that."

"Possibly," Sample said, "you could get that if you sold your stock one or two at a time. How long would that take, Mr. Arbuckle? How much would you spend for feed and care before you sold off all two hundred?"

Peavey got up, walked to the cuspidor and dropped his shredded cigar into it. "Apparently we can't do business, Mrs. Farnum. I'm sorry. But do me the favor of satisfying my curiosity. What do you consider a fair price?"

"Twenty-five thousand dollars," April said without hesitation. "I'll sell for thirty."

Peavey smiled, shook his head and reached for the walking stick he had left propped against the table. "Eight thousand, Mrs. Farnum. Think it over. I'll let that offer stand for ten days.''

"Very well," April said. "I'll let mine stand the same length of time.''

Peavey and Sample exchanged a look. Sample shook his head hopelessly. Peavey suddenly laughed.

"Mrs. Farnum, I'm sorry we're not going to solve our problems," he said. "I like you, Mrs. Farnum.''

He extended his hand across the table to her. She did not take it.

"I don't wish to be rude, Mr. Peavey, but I don't like you.''

Peavey bobbed his head in a curt nod and turned out of the room. Sample snatched up the contract and followed hurriedly. No one got up to show them to the door.

April looked at Link and then at Tom Lawrence. Link tipped back in his chair, hands on table. He met her eyes but said nothing. Tom chuckled softly.

"You might as well have spit in his eye.''

"I considered it.''

"You realize what you're in for?''

"He made it clear enough," April said. "I've got ten days to change my mind. Then he'll give Thorr a free rein.''

Tom Lawrence stared at the table thoughtfully. "I don't like it. There's no way you can fight back. He'll break you, April.''

"We'll see, Tom. I have some plans.''

"I don't like it either," Link said. The front legs of his chair hit the floor noisily. "Thorr's tactics have turned people against Peavey, and they're riding our stages. But that will change if we can't keep schedules. If Thorr hits relay stations, runs off horses, we're bound to have delays. Worse, there's a clause in the mail contract that gives the government the right to cancel if there are 'prolonged and

18

frequent delays in service other than delays resulting from acts of God.' "

Tom nodded somberly. "My guess is they'll hit hard and fast. With public sympathy already in your favor, they've nothing to lose. With you out of business and Peavey & Company the only line on the run, they can say the hell with the public."

"The trouble is we can't fight back," Link said.

"Why not?" April said. "Because I'm a woman?"

There was a silence. Tom Lawrence smiled crookedly and made a gesture that batted the question in Link's direction. Link shrugged uneasily; then he turned in his chair to face April directly.

"You thumbed your nose at Gus Peavey. You have got yourself into a man's kind of war."

"You think I should have accepted his offer?"

"You could have sweet-talked him. He liked you. You could have stalled him along for a while. Maybe after a while you could have got a better price out of him."

"Yes, that would have been the womanly way, wouldn't it?" she said. "Now have you gentlemen more gloom to spread? Or are you ready to hear my plans?"

"Of course," Link said.

"First of all, I want you to option whatever hay the ranchers between here and Augsburg have to sell. All of it. There won't be much; most cattlemen will need all they have for winter feeding. But I want to tie up what's available."

"Wait a minute," Link said. "You're not going to start a hay-burning war?"

"Jim may already have started it. I don't intend to do any more of it unless Thorr does. If that happens, I mean to be sure Peavey & Company is hurt badly."

Tom Lawrence nodded thoughtfully. "It makes

Peavey stations between here and Augsburg especially vulnerable. Thorr could cut his own throat.''

''Also,'' April said, ''I want three relay stations established between here and Star City.''

Link was surprised, but he was quick enough to approve. ''Good. Jim often talked about extending the line north from here. He never got around to it.''

Jim had never quite been able to talk himself into taking the risk, she thought.

Star City and the other mining towns to the north had mushroomed up out of the mountains overnight. Jim hadn't the coaches and the horses to extend his run by another day, and Peavey & Company had got the jump on him. Then they quickly were running on to Augsburg and Adako Falls and were in competition with him. They got most of the through passengers, of course. If Jim was to extend northward successfully, he would have had to woo these passengers away from Peavey, and he was never confident of his ability to do that.

The situation had changed significantly with Jim's death, however. Few people in this part of the country had much doubt that Thorr was responsible. So quite a few travelers were taking Farnum stages as far as Devil's Claw, changing to Peavey only for the last day of the journey. To lengthen the Farnum line as far as Star City now seemed a good gamble.

A gamble, April thought. Everything I'm doing is a gamble. Tom and Link know that and so far they approve. They don't know yet that I'm going to shoot the moon.

She went to a shelf and got the large map she had received from the land office. Tom and Link stood on either side of her to hold it flat as she unrolled it on the table.

20

"Tom, I'm going to ask you to make a trip to Helena," she said. "The territorial legislature is in session, isn't it? I want its permission to operate a toll ferry across the Devil's Claw river."

"Good heavens," Tom said. "There are bridges at all the stage crossings. What point is there to a ferry?"

"Just do it, please. I'll explain later. And I want you to go to the land office and file a preemption claim on this quarter section I've marked here on the map."

Both men leaned close to the map, scowling.

"That's in the middle of the Lost Tribe mountains!" Tom said.

"Not quite in the middle. Will you do that for me?"

"Of course. But I wish you'd make some sense out of it."

"Later. Now there's one thing more. I want a hired gun. A professional who can stand up to those hard cases that Thorr has on his payroll."

Tom Lawrence let go of his end of the map and it rolled up like a Kansas City window shade.

"April," Tom said grimly, "I wish you'd explain what you're up to."

"Oh, cheer up," she said. "I'm not planning to have Thorr assassinated — although I must admit the idea has a certain appeal."

"Then what do you want with a hired killer around? This thing isn't likely to come down to a shooting match."

"I wish I were sure of that, Tom."

"Thorr is not a balanced man," Link said. "If things go against him, you can't tell what he'll do. And they say he goes jig-dancing crazy when he drinks."

"Nobody I know has ever seen him drink," Tom said.

"I hear he does. They say he locks himself up."

"Look here," Tom said. "April's ranch hands are armed. There's a guard at the company barn. Seems to me that's all we need."

"Our boys aren't exactly milksops," April said, "but they're uneasy about the killers Thorr has hanging around. If we had a professional on our side, morale would be better. And there's another thing, Tom. My men are going to get no protection from the law in this county. It seems to me we have to hire our own protection."

"A lot would depend on the man," Tom conceded.

"Of course. I don't want the kind of cat-eye that Thorr hires. I want somebody with brains and judgment."

"And loyalty," Tom said.

"A former lawman — somebody like that."

"Asa Maidenlane," Link said.

The name had a vaguely familiar ring to it; beyond that, it meant nothing to April. Tom, however, recognized it.

"He'll come high," he said.

"Good men do," Link said.

"Is he what we want? He's quick to kill, judging from what I've heard about him."

"I knew him in Dakota when I was driving for Gilmer and Salisbury," Link said. "And you're wrong. He's dead tough, but he's patient, too. Remember the Rome brothers?"

"He brought them in," Tom said.

"Singlehanded. He was shot up some, but neither of the Romes had a scratch on him."

"Do you know where he is now?" April asked.

"Last I knew, he was in the Nations," Link said. "He was working for the Cherokee government, I think. Shall I try to get in touch with him?"

"Do that first thing," April said.

3

JACK THORR TIPPED back in his chair in his private office, feeling the clumsy weight of the big revolver under his coat. Mr. Sample stood before him and Mr. Sample was spluttering mad. Thorr tried to assume an attitude of quiet tolerance by thinking of something else.

Four, he thought. Four bottles. Maybe five.

"Passenger traffic on this run is off forty percent," Sample was saying. "It's off other places, too, where we have competition. Now the boss has come two hundred miles out of his way, on your recommendation, and Mrs. Farnum turned him down flat."

Gus Peavey hadn't even come in to say good-by. He had climbed into his private coach and sent Mr. Sample in. Old Gus must be pretty upset, Thorr thought.

"I'm sorry his feelings is hurt," he muttered.

It was going to happen, he thought. It might have happened after Jim Farnum got himself killed, the damn fool, but it didn't. It hadn't happened now for almost three months, but it was coming on strong and nothing on earth could stop it. Jack Thorr was going to get drunk.

"You did it," Sample said. "You. Nobody else."

"I never denied it. Accidents happen."

Three days, he thought. Five bottles and three days.

"A careless accident. If I'd been the boss, I'd have fired you."

Thorr raised his eyebrows and looked Mr. Sample squarely in the eye. Sample went on quickly.

"At least, I'd have transferred you to another division. You've created a situation here that is well nigh impossible. The pressure must be put on again now, but delicately, shrewdly. I'll be staying in Augsburg for a while. You are not to do anything, not anything, without consulting me.''

"Why didn't Mr. Peavey come in here and tell me this?" Thorr said.

"You're lucky he sent me. He's madder than a hornet."

"You go out there and tell him I want to see him."

"What?"

Thorr let his chair ease forward. He put his hands on his knees as if he were about to get up. "If he wants me took over the carpet, he can come in here and do it himself. Go out there and tell him that."

Sample took a deep breath and stood his ground. "Are you out of your mind, Thorr? I'll do no such thing."

Thorr raised his voice to a roar that could be heard through the closed door to the front office. "Carter!"

Carter Hanford pushed open the door and came in, shotgun in hand. He was short and wiry and wore a business suit. He spent most of his time sitting behind the counter in the front office, the shotgun out of sight but always within reach. He seldom waited on customers, even when the clerk was busy. He did not read or chat with acquaintances or doze. He did not smoke or chew tobacco. He merely sat and waited out the day with the patience of a hunter.

"Go out and tell Mr. Peavey he's needed in here," Thorr said.

Carter Hanford was gone as quickly as he had appeared. Sample turned to stare at a window that was so coated with dust he couldn't see through it. In a moment Gus Peavey stormed in, looking angry and curious and chewing on a fresh cigar.

Thorr got to his feet and extended his hand. "I was

24

afraid I wouldn't get a chance to say good-by.''

Gus Peavey had a Brobdingnagian temper, but he had a trigger on it. He had not parlayed a team of rib-sprung mules into a stage network by stomping and raging until he was sure exactly what stomping and raging would accomplish. He bit down on the cigar and took Thorr's hand.

"Mr. Peavey," Thorr said, "am I on the edge of getting fired?"

Peavey threw a glance at Sample. "Who said anything about firing you?"

"This big-ass little kewpie doll said something about it."

"Sam," Peavey said, "maybe you better leave us alone a minute."

Sample nodded curtly and left the office. Peavey took the cigar out of his mouth, spied out a cuspidor and spat in that general direction.

"Now look here," he said. "I'm mad. I'm mad at Mrs. Farnum, at myself, at Sam Sample and at the first son of a bitch I see when I step outside. Things have gone wrong on this division. You're the superintendent, so I'm mad at you. But I'm not thinking of firing you. Let's get that straight."

Thorr sat down again and tipped back the chair. "Someday there will be something to be done that will look bad. You'll want it done but you'll have to fire me after I do it. We both know that can happen. But I won't have no squeaky-jaw lawyer around reminding me all the time."

"I don't blame you," Peavey said. "It's my fault. I gave him a dressing down. Then I sent him in here and he passed it on to you."

"He said you came here on my recommendation. The way it was, he wrote and asked me if I thought the Farnum woman would sell. I wrote back that I thought she might, that's all."

"Well, you sure misread her."

"She's a woman."

Peavey allowed himself a small smile. "Yes. A very handsome woman, younger than I expected. And tough. A very tough woman."

"No," Thorr said, squinting thoughtfully. "Not tough. The young and pretty ones have always had things come easy to them, and they ain't tough."

"Don't misread her again, Jack."

"Well, she's a woman. I don't guarantee nothing in that department."

"Sample might be of help to you there. He'll be in Augsburg. Consult him."

"No," Thorr said. "You want him to run this division, make him superintendent."

"I said consult him. That doesn't mean you have to take orders from him."

"He don't see it that way."

"He will. I'll speak to him. He can be of use to you. He'll handle the sheriff, for one thing."

"That's fine, Mr. Peavey. But I'm telling you flat out. He tries to handle me, I'll throw him out the window. Any orders has got to come from you."

"All right," Peavey said. "I'll give you one right now. I want Farnum schedules disrupted. I don't have to spell that out. But I don't want any more stupidity like going into a man's home to beat him up. If that sort of thing is necessary, it should happen in a saloon, on the street, and it should be done by strangers. It should look like a street fight. It should look accidental, casual. Everything that happens should look like an accident."

Thorr nodded his acceptance of that. Hell, he thought, Old Gus can't fire me, not now. He needs a lot more dirty work done. If he has to make a choice, I'm more important to him than Sample.

"You keep a sharp eye on the Farnum woman," Peavey said, "and on that manager of hers, too. They're up to something, and I want to know what."

Peavey made a point of shaking hands again before he left. Thorr found a scrap of paper and a pencil. He made a large figure 5 and under it he wrote "Right now." He left the building by a back door and was in the yard between the office and the Peavey barn. Sid Luna and Frisco Hays were pitching horseshoes beside the barn. Thorr folded the paper several times and gave it to Luna.

"Dolly?" Luna said.

Thorr's look reproached him for asking a question he knew the answer to. "Anybody asks where I'm at, you don't know. Maybe I went to Star City, maybe Augsburg."

4

DOLLY NEVADA MET Sid Luna in the hall, took the note from him and saw him to the door. Unfolding the note and glancing at it, she went into the parlor. Queenie and Patsy were playing dominoes and eating taffy. Tessie was on the sofa, lying on her stomach and buffing her nails. Beulah, the black housekeeper, prowled the room with a fly swatter in hand.

Dolly crumpled the note and threw it into the fireplace, aware that the others all knew who had brought it and what it meant. Beulah broke the silence.

"You going to be gone, Miss Dolly?"

"Couple days, maybe three. You're the boss-lady till I get back. Anybody gives you any sass, you let me know."

"Nobody sasses Beulah, Miss Dolly," Beulah said, a soft challenge in her voice.

"That's right," Tessie said cheerfully from the sofa. "You wore-out old black witch."

Beulah's laugh was a merry squeal. "I'm twice as old as you and half as wore out."

"Tell Andrew to bring the buggy round," Dolly said. "I'm going to change."

"Into your fighting clothes?" Tessie said.

Beulah struck out with the fly swatter and smacked Tessie soundly on the backside.

"Hey!"

"You watch your mouth," Beulah said.

Dolly went upstairs and changed into a serge skirt and a slightly worn basque. There was no point in dressing fancy for Jack Thorr; whatever she wore might very well get torn.

She took two carpetbags from a closet, quickly stuffed

28

extra unmentionables and toilet articles into one, and went down the back stairs to the kitchen, where she packed bacon, eggs, beans and coffee. She unlocked the liquor cabinet, took five bottles of Monongahela from it, and added these to her baggage. Beulah came into the kitchen, and Dolly gave her the key to the cabinet.

"Buggy's all ready," Beulah said. "Why you do it, Miss Dolly?"

"He owns this house. I guess he owns me."

"Last time you come home all banged up. We had to call the doctor."

"That was time before last. Last time wasn't so bad."

"Truth is, you're scared not to go."

"I'd hate to have him mad at me sober," Dolly admitted. "Besides, who'd take care of him? You look after things here and don't worry about Dolly."

"Yes, ma'am. Any crazies show up, I'll send for Deputy Beasely."

"If that loco sheepherder shows up with his hand bellows, don't fiddle around getting a deputy. You Mickey Finn him quick."

"I druther kiss that slooney with the shot bag. I'd enjoy it."

"Whatever," Dolly said.

She went out and got into the buggy beside Andrew, a two-hundred-pound man with red hair and a scraggly red beard. He had been stomped by a horse when he was twelve years old and hadn't been right since. He was moose strong but docile enough unless somebody teased him, as Thorr sometimes did. He did simple chores, and Dolly and the girls looked after him. Few people knew that he was Dolly's younger brother.

They drove north out of town on the stage road, passing the gate of the Farnum ranch. A few minutes later they swung west on a side road, crossed a bridge over a creek, passed a farmhouse. The road dwindled to a trace, hardly more than a trail, as it climbed into the mountains. It climbed steeply, descended, then snaked up to a shelflike summit spotted with brush and juniper and jack pine. Thorr's cabin was here, backed up against a spring and a rock outcropping.

Andrew halted the horse a little distance from the door, and they got out of the buggy. He dragged the sash weight that he used as a tie iron from the buggy, dropped it and snapped tie rope to headstall. Moving with a patent reluctance, he carried Dolly's carpetbags to the cabin. She produced a key and took the padlock off the door, hooking it into the staple on the jamb and leaving it there. Andrew turned silently back toward the buggy. He was sad today, she thought. He didn't like Jack Thorr, and he didn't like her coming here.

"Go straight home," she said. "Do as Beulah says now."

He turned slowly and threw one question-word at her. "When?"

"Thursday afternoon. You don't have to remember. Beulah will tell you."

The cabin air was a blend of stale smells, each with its harsh tinge of memory. She left the door ajar and swung open the small window. The place had been tidied since she was here last. Whether Jack sent someone to clean up the mess or whether he came and did it himself, she didn't know.

Sunlight was interrupted early by mountains to the west, and it was cool here. She filled the cookstove from a woodbox, splashed in kerosene from a three-gallon can under the sink and quickly had a fire humming. She filled a bucket at the spring and got water heating. She sliced

30

bacon, put cold biscuits into the oven to warm. Jack would be stone sober when he arrived. She would try to get some bacon and eggs into him before the demon took over.

He didn't drink in saloons — at least nothing more than buttermilk. He didn't drink anywhere but here. Sometime, somewhere, long ago, he had faced the truth about himself and his demon. So when he drank, he shut himself up with the demon. And with a woman. In a way, you had to give him credit. But it was hell on Dolly Nevada.

She had been with Jack Thorr for twelve years. She had kept house for him at first and lived with him as his wife. He had been strange in his lovemaking and sometimes cruel, but she hadn't had to look after him when he holed up on a drunk. There had been another woman for that, and then another; Dolly never let herself wonder what had happened to them.

They had been from the little band of women that he always kept near him, women that he bought and sold and traded and who gave him their earnings. In return, he gave them spending money and housed and clothed and fed them, and that was enough for them. They were content with their lives, and Dolly understood their contentment.

Before she ever became his woman, Dolly had made Jack promise that Andrew could be with her. For a time, resentfully, Jack put up with him; but as Andrew grew older and sensed that he was somehow different from other people, he grew more difficult. He resented Jack, and Jack knew it and enjoyed prodding him. Dolly lived in constant dread of the day when her brother's thick crust of patience would crack. She might have felt humiliated when Jack put her in charge of one of his houses, but she didn't. Andrew went with her and she felt only relief.

Twelve years. A lifetime, she thought. I must look forty-five and I think like it and act like it. My God, am I really only twenty-eight?

She was lighting a lantern when she heard Jack's horse snorting after the climb up the hill. She went to the door to watch as he unsaddled and staked the horse in a patch of grass. He came into the cabin with no word of greeting, no embrace. He went to her luggage and took out the whiskey, setting the bottles in a row on a shelf. Then he took one of them to the table and sat down. She handed him a corkscrew and he drew the cork. He tipped the bottle high and drank like a hungry foal.

"Got to be in Augsburg Friday morning," he said.

"Sure, lover."

"You see I make it."

"Sure."

She got bacon frying, broke eggs into the pan. He tipped the bottle again, hitting it hard. She tried to plan the next three days in her mind. By Thursday morning the booze would be gone. She'd flush him out with coffee and spring water, shave him and clean him up, get a meal into him, get him on a horse.

"For Christ's sake," he said, "what're you doing?"

"Cooking. We'll eat something. It will give you a foundation."

"I ain't hungry."

He came over and handed her the bottle. She raised it and took a small drink. He reached for the bottle with one hand and the frying pan with the other. He slid the pan off the stove and slammed it against the wall.

"I ain't hungry."

She put down a surge of panic. She had hoped he would drink quietly at first and then talk a while before he started throwing things around. If the talking part came first, it seemed to her that he was less violent later.

"Off to the races," she said, as he reached for her.

5

"WE BEGIN THE run to Star City tomorrow," April told Tom Lawrence. "Notices were posed all along the line today. I think we've caught the Peavey people by surprise."

She was seated in her living room with Link Arbuckle and Tom. Link had got back from Star City yesterday. Tom had just arrived this evening after a full two weeks in Helena. Since they were both bachelors, April had invited them to supper, which she had cooked and served with the aid of Sally Smithwick. She had arranged with Sally to stay on with her as companion and housekeeper, and this was a great convenience.

Tom looked even more rumpled than usual. He swished his brandy around in its glass and then sloughed it down at a gulp. "You set up three stations and stocked them without Thorr catching on?"

Link grinned smugly. "I found three hungry little ranchers in just the right places. A crew from April's ranch drove fifty head of horses north last week. We're all set."

"Heaven knows what Thorr's reaction will be," Tom said, "but it will be dirty."

"I expect we'll get more of what we've been getting," Link said.

"Somebody has been sabotaging our coaches," April explained. "We've lost wheels on the road, brakes have been tampered with — that sort of thing. We've had no serious accidents, just delays and inconvenience. It's all happened near Augsburg, and Link thinks he knows who's doing it."

"Just a hunch," Link said. "Thorr was in Augsburg a week or so ago. He also spent some time at McCabe station. I'm guessing that Ike McCabe is the culprit."

"The sheriff is no help, of course," April said. "We need a security man of our own, somebody who can put the fear of God into people like McCabe."

"I wrote to Asa Maidenlane in care of the Cherokee government," Link said. "I've heard nothing."

Sally came in and refilled their coffee cups. Tom went around with the brandy bottle. April, a little surprised at herself, accepted a second glass. Then Tom gave a report of his activities in Helena.

He'd filed a preemption claim on the land April wanted. She was now in control of it and would have a patented deed in six month's time.

He had also persuaded the territorial legislature to grant her the right to operate a toll ferry across the Devil's Claw river. This had been done by means of a short paragraph tucked into an omnibus bill that the legislature passed just before it adjourned. Tom had brought back certified copies.

"It's all in order," he assured them. "I just wish I knew what it's all about."

"You should have guessed," April said. "Both of you."

"I'm afraid to guess," Link said.

It was time to explain. She was feeling the brandy and she hoped she wouldn't be overly dramatic.

"I have another surprise for Peavey," she said. "A big one. I've got in touch with an old friend of Jim's, an engineer named Pete Lafortune. He arrived here three days ago. He's going to build a shortcut over the Lost Tribe mountains."

Link took a deep breath and blew it out noisily. Tom Lawrence poured his brandy into his coffee and refilled his glass from the bottle.

"April," Tom said, "there is no way over the Lost Tribes."

"But there is. That's the point."

"April —"

"Hear her out," Link said. He was frowning hard. "Jim once hinted — I'm trying to remember."

"There's a way and it's really quite easy, once you find it," April said. "Jim once took me over it. We crossed the range and came out on the stage road just below McCabe station. It took us around three hours and a half, traveling leisurely. With a decent road and a relay station at the summit, a stagecoach could do better than that.

"Do you see what that means? We can cut out that whole long loop south around the end of the range. We can make the run to Augsburg in around four hours instead of twelve. We can eliminate Augsburg as an overnight stop. We can cut the trip from here to Adako Falls from three days to two."

Link leaned forward in his chair. "The runs between Augsburg and the Falls are fairly short now, and that's mostly flat plateau country. If the shortcut's as good as you say, yes, we could make the whole trip in two long runs."

"Slow down," Tom said. "If you can do it, so can Peavey."

"The only possible river crossing is on the claim you took out for me," April said.

"The road will be a public road. You can't deny it to Peavey coaches just because it crosses your land."

"I also will be operating the ferry."

"You can't deny him use of that either."

"I can set the toll for stagecoaches higher than Old Baldy."

Tom blinked slowly. He looked at Link. They both laughed.

"Glory come to meetin'!" Tom said. "You just might make this work."

"Of course it will work," she said. "And you needn't look so amazed."

"But this route over the Lost Tribes," Link said. "I can't quite believe it."

"I can't either," Tom said. "This engineer you've got — is he any good?"

"The best."

"He's been over the route?"

"Not yet," she admitted.

Tom wagged his head tiredly. His longish, graying hair was mussed and hung down over his ears. "Then how can you be sure —?"

"Because Jim said so. He had it in the back of his head to build the road some day, I think."

"I want to see this route," Link said. "I want to ride over it."

"I'll take you both over it," April said. "Pete Lafortune is in Augsburg now. He's hiring a crew and getting together the teams and equipment he'll need. He's going to start preliminary work on the Augsburg side of the range right away. I showed him on a map where to begin. He'll be back here next week, and we'll make the trip."

It all sounds crazy and mixed up to them, she thought. I'm not going about this in the way a man would go about it, and they can't quite accept me. They want to accept me, bless their hearts, but only man-thinking makes sense to them.

36

"It may seem strange that Pete Lafortune is starting work without having been over the route," she said, "but there's a good reason. I started to take him over it, but two riders were following us, so we turned back. They were that pair that is always hanging around the Peavey barn, pitching horseshoes."

"Hays and Luna," Link said.

"Anyway, Pete knew Jim. He said that if Jim believed a road could be built, it could be built . . . . Really, it will be simple. You'll see. There's only one bad grade the whole way."

A door slammed at the back of the house. There were voices in the kitchen. Sally came in, followed by a man with hat in hand, a lean-hard man with a ropy grace about him. He was in trail clothes, sweat-stained and dusty. He had thick yellow hair blazed with white, and his eyes were blue with a smile behind them.

"Someone to see you, Link," Sally said.

Link was already on his feet, hand extended in greeting.

"Ace!"

"Hello, Link."

They held a handshake a moment, sharing a steady look, wasting no words. Sally unobtrusively left the room. Link turned to the others.

"Mrs. Farnum, Tom Lawrence, this is Asa Maidenlane."

April offered him her hand. He took it as he would take a man's hand, firmly and fully and without awkwardness. The contact summoned a half-forgotten stirring in her, and she quickly withdrew her fingers. It must be the brandy, she thought.

"Sit down, Mr. Maidenlane. Have you had supper?"

"I'll get something at the hotel," he said. He shook hands with Tom Lawrence, then he removed a gunbelt,

37

placed it and his hat on a sofa and sat down beside them.

A gunman. A killer. It seemed important to April to remind herself of that.

"I'll fix you something," she said. "It will just take a moment."

"Please sit still," he said. "I'd rather eat later."

She had started to get up. She sank back in her chair.

"I expected a letter, Ace," Link said. "Your being here is better. We need you right now."

"The Cherokees fired me," Asa Maidenlane said. "You ought to know that before you take me on."

"Fired you, Ace? Why?"

"I shot up a deputy U.S. marshal."

"You're not on the run?"

"No."

Sally came in with the coffee pot and a cup, which she set at Asa Maidenlane's elbow and filled. Tom handed him the brandy bottle and he laced the coffee liberally.

"I'd like to know what happened," April said.

"I had a prisoner, a Cherokee. The deputy marshal tried to take him from me. In the Nations, jurisdiction is often unclear. The deputy marshal fired first. There were witnesses. There was a hearing at Fort Smith. The judge exonerated me."

"But the Cherokees fired you."

"They're trying to run their own nation, but Washington breathes hard on them. After I tangled with a Federal man, they had to let me go. They also paid me a bonus."

There was a silence while he sipped his coffee. A terse man, April thought, but with a mellow quality, too, and a quiet reserve of energy. He's younger than I expected, she thought. He's no older than Link.

"They say your price is high, Mr. Maidenlane," she said.

"What do you pay your drivers?"

"Three dollars a day."

"That will do for me."

She had expected to pay much more, and she was startled. Link's dark eyes sought her approval, then he said, "That's small pay for risky work, Ace."

"There was a time when I wanted to get rich at it. That's past."

Tom Lawrence was amused. "You don't want to get rich?"

"Three dollars a day," Asa Maidenlane said, a smile touching his eye corners. "If I need more, I'll ask for it."

"We're beginning a new run north tomorrow," April said. "Can you ride along?"

"Yes, but fill me in. What kind of trouble do you expect?"

She gestured uncertainly. "I hope, none. But Peavey's people are ruthless. The law gives us no protection. We have to establish our own. It won't be easy."

"I know," he said. "Jack Thorr is here."

"You know him?"

"He and I go back to track-laying days. He was a troublebuster for the U.P. I was a county deputy."

"You were friends?"

"No," Asa Maidenlane said.

6

THE FIRST FARNUM coach for Star City was scheduled to leave at seven-thirty A.M., half an hour later than the Peavey coach. April didn't want the drivers to get into a race, she explained.

She chose old Sam Case to drive this first trip. He was almost seventy and didn't drive regularly anymore but worked at the ranch training coachers. He was a whip in the oldtime tradition, with a flair of speech and dress that younger drivers tried to imitate. He showed up in Wellington boots, a buckskin shirt, beaded gauntlets and a new black Stetson with silver worked into the braiding of the *barbiquejo*. And a jawful of flatback. Sam had been known to brag that he could spit the length of a six-horse hitch from the driver's seat and nick the off pointer in whichever ear he chose — against the wind.

Asa Maidenlane rode beside him on the box of the line's best Abbott & Downing coach, specially shined up for the occasion. Link Arbuckle rode inside with the paying passengers. Since the new service had been announced only the day before, there were only three of these — the local Methodist minister, his wife, and a windmill salesman who had a hangover and had missed the Peavey coach.

At almost the last moment, April had an impulse to go along, and she gave in to it.

"I'll ride as far as the halfway station," she announced. "I'll catch the southbound there and be back here this evening."

Link tried to talk her out of it, pointing out that they'd

caught Thorr off guard and he was apt to act hastily and viciously.

"He could very well figure that a breakdown on this first trip will give our new service a bad name," Link said. He added, "It would, too."

"If there's trouble, I want to be there," she insisted, and she hurried home for a hat and a veil.

A little breathless, she settled herself beside the minister's wife. Sam Case yelled, "Hi!" The horses pressed into their harness, and the stage surged forward like a thing afloat, swinging gently on its thoroughbraces. A few rods down the street Jack Thorr watched from the Peavey & Company doorway. April saw his look of detached and casual inspection explode into unguarded astonishment as he recognized the man beside the driver. She looked back to see him standing on the boardwalk, squinting after them.

They were quickly in open country. Ranch hands were gathered at the Farnum gate to wave and cheer as the coach rolled past. April fell into conversation with the minister and his wife. The drummer sprawled on the rear seat and snored. The road spun up the long and creek-veined valley, bending with the land. After awhile it lifted into low hills, placid satellites of the bold range to the west.

This was a land of sage and bunch grass, rolling but sometimes cut by sharp, rocky draws. Now and then there were cottonwoods with cattle lying in their dappled shade, and sometimes on distant hilltops there were stands of spruce and pine. The coach occasionally passed small ranches. Once in a while there was a neat cabin and well-kept barnyard, more often an untidy melee of sheds and shacks that looked as if they'd blow away in the next high wind. This was cattle country spattered with one-bucket operators who shared range and water, helped one another when they weren't stealing from one another, made bank loans when they could and managed to hang on by their toenails.

Buckley station was a ranch sixteen miles out of Devil's Claw, veiled from the road by a grove of cottonwoods. The original homesteader had worked and worried himself to death trying to provide for a slovenly wife and seven children. His widow was now married to a windy fribbler named Oc Buckley who knew little about ranching, cared less, was in no danger of working himself to death and had her pregnant again. Link had his doubts about Oc as a stationmaster, but the Buckleys were eager for the business, were in the right place and had a large barn. The only other ranch in the vicinity was already serving as a Peavey station, and there was hardly time to build a station from scratch and staff it with people he was more sure of.

The coach slowed, made the turn into the side road and wound among the cottonwoods. At this point, when there was yet no clear view of the buildings, April knew that disaster awaited them here, knew it with a certainty that brought her forward to lean on the window ledge. Afterward, she realized that the smell of smoke hung among the trees and that some discriminating sense told her it was not smoke from a chimney. Quickly they were in the yard, and she was looking at a rectangle of smoking black and gray rubble where the barn had been.

A small boy stood near it, sweating in its heat, poking with a pole. When he saw the stage, he ran toward the house, calling. Oc Buckley plunged through the doorway, and the rest of his family poured after him.

Oc was slightly built, bald and had a blond mustache

42

waxed into hornlike points. He wore a ragged undershirt, trousers that were screwed around to one side and carpet slippers. His wife was a large woman in a long shapeless garment that might have been either dress or nightgown or both. Thin reddish hair hung unevenly to her shoulders. Oc had a frying pan in his hand, holding it as he would a weapon.

"They hit us at first light!" he bellowed, hopping with excitement and waving the frying pan as the coach came to a stop. "Wasn't out of bed yet when they come down on us!"

Link was the first out of the coach. April followed him.

"Who?" Link demanded.

"Desperados!" Mrs. Buckley said. "They was a-waving firearms and a-blaspheming!"

"And a-burning and a-ravaging!" Oc seemed to be swatting imaginary enemies with the frying pan. "They come like the Four Horsemen of the Apocalypse!"

"How many were there?" Link asked.

"Two. Leastways, that was all I seen."

"Two big ones!" Mrs. Buckley said. She was as flushed with excitement as her husband. Both seemed thoroughly but cheerfully disoriented. "They was masked over their faces. All of a sudden there they was in the bedroom. They tied us to the bed and padlocked the kids into the storeroom. Kids took the door off the hinges and come and unreleased us."

"By that time," Oc said, "the barn was a-blazing to make hell look like a glowworm! The oldest boy was a-running in and out a-trying to save stuff and about to get himself crisped. Cal, I said, ain't no use a-panicking. Might as well back off and watch her go!"

"He did save some stuff," a leggy girl about twelve said.

"What about the horses?" Link said.

"They run 'em off — your coachers, leastways. I got five saddle horses in the far pasture they never seen. But you ain't going to get no relief team today, folks. Not at Buckley station!"

The preacher and his wife had been staring at the rubble. They now came up behind Oc, who was startled — or made out to be — and made a defensive gesture with the frying pan. The preacher's wife seemed amused.

"What," she said, "is the frying pan for?"

"They took our weapons!" Oc said as if that were a sensible answer that should have been obvious. "If they hadn't took our weapons, it would have been a different story around here!"

"Why didn't you go after the horses?" Link said. "You have saddle ponies."

"We didn't have no weapons! Besides, they was long gone by the time —"

"Cal did go after them," the leggy girl said.

Oc granted the child a tolerant look. Then he looked around at the rest of his family anxiously. "Where's Cal at?"

"I ain't noticed him," Mrs. Buckley said. "Desdemona, you mean he — ?"

"The lean-to wasn't on fire yet, and he threw out the saddles — and the harness, too. Then he caught his blue roan and went after the desperados."

"That boy!" Oc said. "He should have told me. We'd've planned it out."

April was spitting mad by this time. She took a deep breath and told herself to keep her mouth shut, at least till she knew what she was going to say. If she opened it, she was going to bawl out somebody or everybody and maybe make no more sense than Oc Buckley. She was furious

44

with Link for putting Oc in charge here, with the preacher's wife because she seemed amused and with Asa Maidenlane and Sam Case because they were leaning against the coach looking unconcerned and talking calmly as if just passing the time of day. It was the hungover drummer who provided the last straw by climbing out of the coach, looking around anxiously and asking, "Did the privy go up, too?"

She let go then, turning to Asa Maidenlane and addressing herself to him.

"There's no point in standing around like helpless ninnies, is there? Here's what we're going to do. Asa — Mr. Maidenlane — you and Link —"

"Folks call me Ace."

"Do they?" she said, unable to keep sarcasm out of her voice. "Well, Ace, you and Link catch a couple of those saddle horses and go after the coachers. Thorr's men probably just scattered them in the hills. If you start right now, maybe you can get a team rounded up by the time the southbound comes through this afternoon."

"That's not going to get this coach to Star City on time," he said.

"Well, there's not much we can do about that, is there?"

"Seems like there might be."

"Sam," she said, "can these horses make the halfway station?"

"At a walk and a rest every few miles," Sam said, "they might make it. It'll take the rest of the day. We can figure on Star City about midnight."

"Then that's what we'll have to figure on. But at least we can try to get the southbound into Devil's Claw on time." Asa Maidenlane was still leaning against the coach, and she glared at him. "*Can't* we, Asa?"

45

"Ace," he said.

"Ace, then!"

Her eyes skewered him, demanding an answer. He took off his hat and brushed back his pinto hair with his forearm. Hold on, she told herself. Don't scream at him. Swear at him, fire him, but don't scream.

"April," he said, satisfaction in his tone as if something between them had been settled. "We'll get both coaches through, April. On time."

"What?" she said. She kept her glare on him but the fire was out of it, and she no longer wanted to scream. Then there was a distraction as the girl called Desdemona cried out and pointed toward a low rise just beyond the house.

"Cal!"

A tall boy had appeared, on foot, limping, carrying a saddle on his shoulder. Desdemona ran to meet him, and the other children followed her.

He limped into the yard and put down the saddle. He was about sixteen, April guessed, a skinny kid whose shirt and jeans were too small for him. One side of his face was bruised and swollen, the eye almost closed. There was a crust of blood under the other eye, and his lips were split and puffy. He looked over the group narrowly, ignoring Oc's petulant questions, and addressed himself to Maidenlane.

"The whoreson bastards shot my horse."

Oc swung the frying pan viciously at the boy's head. "You watch your foul mouth!"

The boy dodged easily but narrowly, caught his stepfather's arm, appropriated the frying pan and flung it over the stagecoach into the cottonwoods.

Oc was not silenced even momentarily. "I apologize

46

for this boy, Mrs. Farnum. He's nothing but trouble to me.''

"Shut up!" April said. She moved close to the boy and gently touched his bruised face. "Someone get some water and a towel."

The boy drew back from her. "I'm all right."

"What happened, son?" Asa Maidenlane said.

"They shot Blue Boy out from under me. Then they beat me up. They said I was lucky they had orders not to kill nobody. I give one of 'em a nose bleed."

"All right, son." Maidenlane's big hand cupped Cal's shoulder. "You forget that. If anybody comes asking, including the law, they still had masks on. You wouldn't know them if your life depended on it."

"Hell," the boy said. "They was those two duded up gun-toters that hang around the Peavey barn in Devil's Claw. I ain't scared of the sneaking bastards."

"There might come a time for you to identify them in court. That will be the time not to be scared. Until then, you get scared and stay that way."

The boy gave a small nod. "After they beat me up, I followed 'em on foot. They didn't see me. They drove your horses across Bear Creek and into Wagon Wheel Canyon. You know the country around here?"

"No."

"Well, that canyon branches up into three canyons. I suppose they split up the horses and drove 'em up all three."

Mrs. Buckley called Cal over to the porch, where she had a basin of water and a cloth, and she went to work cleaning up his face. Asa Maidenlane followed, talking quietly with the boy.

"That boy!" Oc said for the tenth time. "He gets

himself into more kinds of trouble than a kitty-cat with a ball of yarn and a piece of flypaper.''

"Mr. Buckley," April said. "We'll put up some kind of temporary shelter here for our horses — a crude sort of pavilion, don't you think, Link? Then we'll help you rebuild your barn. But let me tell you, I'll take that boy anytime. If it weren't for him, I'd pull this station out from under you and build one down the road. You think about that."

She turned to Link. "Now I want you and Mr. Buckley and Ace to saddle up three of those ponies in Mr. Buckley's pasture and get started after our horses."

"We'll need all four," Asa Maidenlane said, coming toward them from the porch. Cal followed him, holding a cloth against his swollen face. "One for Cal. And you two will have to round up the coachers by yourselves. The kid and I have another errand."

"Will you *please* — " April began. He was counter-manding her orders, she thought. He was actually taking over. And yet she sensed that this was not the time for an icy assertion of her authority. There was a balance of sureness and rashness about this man that she had missed. And there was something else, something odd that had to do with the gentle way he spoke her name and with three dollars a day and with a remote smile not quite released. She said mildly, "What errand, Ace?"

"Cal tells me the Peavey station isn't much more than half a mile up the road. We need a fresh hitch."

He looked from one to another, giving them time to grasp his simple and direct intention.

He knew at once what he was going to do, April thought. Old Sam Case no doubt knew it, too.

"The Finchleens run that station," Link said. "Three men, a woman."

48

· · ·

A few minutes later, Maidenlane and Cal reined off the stage road and up a low, brush-spotted slope. Just below its summit, they dismounted, tied the horses to low-growing juniper and went ahead on foot. From the top, peering over a clump of brush, they had a view of Finchleen station.

It was a well-kept place with a creek running behind it and making a horseshoe turn so that the station was almost on an island. The barn was in the foreground, a huge building with the creek running across a fenced pasture behind it. The house was built against a slope upstream from the barn. It was a long log building with a porch all the way across its front.

There were two men working at a forge beside the barn, shoeing a horse. They were one of the Finchleen brothers and a hired hand, Cal said. Two saddled horses were tied to a hitchrail in front of the house. They were two hundred yards away, but Cal was certain they belonged to the two men who had beaten him up.

THE INTERIOR OF Finchleen station was one large, long room with a stove and sink at one end of it and a bar built out of packing cases at the other. In between were several tables and chairs, cowhides scattered around as rugs, two cuspidors, a china cabinet and two bunks. There was a big stone fireplace beside the bar and on the other side of that, a brass bedstead.

Bart Finchleen went behind the bar for a bottle and two glasses and took them over to the table where his two guests were eating bacon and eggs.

"How about a snort of whiskey with that breakfast?"

"I guess not," Sid Luna said.

"On the house."

"Get thee behind me, Satan," Frisco Hays said. "On the other hand, man does not live by bread alone. I could use about three fingers."

Hays had a swollen nose that he kept touching with his left hand as he ate. Finchleen poured a generous three fingers of whiskey into one of the glasses. Hays tossed it down at a gulp and motioned for a refill.

"Always turn the other cheek," he said.

"Whoa up," Luna said. "You know how the boss feels about drinking on the job."

"Screw him. He seeth not the mote in his own eye."

"Besides," Luna said, "he said to come straight back to Devil's Claw. We come in smelling like whiskey, he'll know damn well we didn't."

"Coming here was your idea."

"We been up all night. I'm not up to any more time in the saddle on an empty stomach. Besides, you got a busted nose. That gives us an excuse."

"It isn't busted," Hays said.

"It's sure swole up."

Hays drank half the whiskey in his glass and chased it with a sip of coffee. Luna eyed Bart Finchleen narrowly.

"Anybody asks, we wasn't here."

"Bear a little false witness," Hays said.

"I've seen nobody but the passengers on the morning stage," Finchleen assured them.

"What about your woman, the others?" Luna said.

"Likewise." Finchleen raised his voice to reach the woman busy at the kitchen end of the house. "Eileen, bring these gents more coffee."

Finchleen was worried. There was a stage feud on, and he was likely to be in the middle of it. He knew these men only slightly, but they worked for Jack Thorr and so did he. They were very likely responsible for the column of smoke that had risen from the Buckley place at daylight this morning. The barn, he guessed, but he wasn't going to ask, and Eileen knew better than to mention it, too. These were clearly men that the Finchleens wanted to stay on the good side of.

Eileen brought over the coffeepot. She was a gaunt woman with heavy eyebrows and a darkness in her face. As she refilled the cups, there was the sound of someone on the porch. The front door opened, and Cal Buckley came into the station.

Luna was immediately on his feet. Hays leaned to one side in his chair. Both had hands on their gun butts. Cal stopped in his tracks as if as startled as they were. He spread his arms, holding his hands away from his body.

"I got no gun. I'm here friendly. I didn't know —"

Bart Finchleen had little use for the Buckleys, except for this kid, whom he liked. But there was clearly a quarrel

51

here; it seemed important to show Hays and Luna where his sympathy lay.

"What the hell you want?" he demanded.

"I come to buy a drink of your whiskey."

Eileen moved closer to the boy, peering at his bruised face. "Cal, what happened to you?"

"Fell off a horse."

Luna sat down, his hand still on his gun. Hays picked up his fork but kept his eyes on the boy.

"You need doctoring," Eileen said.

"Ma already did that. I want a drink of whiskey."

"Haven't you any whiskey at your place?"

Cal managed a grin, one-sided and swollen. "We can't keep it, not with Oc around."

"Give him a drink, Bart," she said.

"No, sir," Bart said. "I'm not serving a kid."

Luna turned his chair sideways to the table so he was facing the bar squarely. "Give him a drink. I'll buy it."

Bart Finchleen went around the bar and set a glass on it. Cal walked up and laid a dollar on the bar.

"I said I'll buy it," Luna said.

"No offense," Cal said, "but I'll buy my own."

"On the house," Bart said.

"Keep out of this," Luna said. "Pour."

Finchleen poured a small drink into the glass.

"More," Luna said.

Finchleen poured a full three fingers.

"Keep pouring. Fill it up."

"Wait a minute," Eileen said. "This boy maybe never had a drink in his life. You want to kill him?"

"Accidents happen," Luna said. He drew his gun and laid it on the table to his right. It was pointed more toward Hays than Hays liked. He reached out with his fork and moved it an inch.

52

Cal watched as Bart Finchleen slowly filled the glass. It was coming out wrong, he thought. He'd drink the damn whiskey, if it came to that, but Luna's gun was on the table and that was wrong.

Keep them looking at you with their backs to the back door, Asa Maidenlane had said. Keep their attention — put on a show if you have to, but don't prod them into drawing guns. I don't want to shoot anybody if I can avoid it, and I don't want to get shot.

Cal picked up the full glass. "You think I'm scared to drink this?" he said, looking at Luna.

"Straight down," Luna said.

The back door, which was at the kitchen end of the house, opened. The hired hand, whose name was Fred, and George Finchleen came in. George and Bart were brothers. They were both lean and slow moving and would have looked enough alike to be twins except that George wore glasses. Luna and Hays turned, touching their guns out of long habit that was partly caution, partly show-off, relaxing again as they recognized the newcomers. They didn't see the third man just outside the door. Bart Finchleen, who was behind the bar, saw that somebody was there and craned his neck to see who; then he caught his brother's frown and little shake of head, and he looked down at the bar.

George and Fred walked slowly toward the bar. Maidenlane came in the door behind them, revolver in hand. Bart Finchleen moved down the bar a bit so as not to be in line with Hays and Luna. Cal's hand shook as he raised the glass, spilling a little of the liquor. He touched the glass to his lips, felt the scalding whiskey on his tongue.

"Straight down, damn it," Luna said.

He touched the gun on the table beside him, and

53

Maidenlane fired. The shot missed Luna's fingers by a hair, sweeping the revolver off the table and spinning it across the floor.

Luna sprang to his feet, half-turning. Cal lunged and got him in the eyes with the whiskey. As Luna's hands went to his face, Cal reached back behind himself and launched a bale-buster that landed just above the belt buckle. Luna doubled up, groaning loudly, and the kid sledged him on the back of the head and brought a knee into his face at the same time.

"Easy," Maidenlane said. "Ease off, son."

But even as Luna hit the floor, Cal was around the end of the table and on Hays, sweeping the man's plate up and hard against his damaged nose, tipping him over backward in his chair. Left-handed, the boy snatched Hays's revolver from its holster as he fell and gun-barreled him as he landed. He drove a rib-cracking kick into Hays's side, stepped back and addressed himself to the two gasping, semi-conscious bodies before him.

"That there was for Blue Boy."

He picked up Luna's weapon and went behind the bar beside Bart Finchleen and leaned forward on his elbows to cover the group with a gun in each hand. They looked at the boy's bruised face and understood that some kind of a score had been settled and they bore him no malice, although they might have to pretend to. Eileen got hold of a chair and sank into it. Bart turned to Maidenlane and asked the most intelligent question he could think of.

"What the hell?"

"How many fresh coach horses you got?" Maidenlane asked.

Bart had to think a moment. "Two full teams. A couple of extra wheelers."

"Peavey & Company owes them to us, Mr. Finchleen

Our coach will pull up here any minute and will take a fresh hitch. Then we'll drive our team and a fresh one for the afternoon southbound back to Buckley station. You men can help.''

Bart looked at his brother, and there was understanding between them. They were caught in a stage war, and they would do what a man with a gun told them. But they had to make at least some small show of reluctance.

"And if we refuse?" Bart said.

"We'll burn your barn," Maidenlane said.

8

ON THE LONG stage ride from Augsburg, Mr. Sample did a good deal of thinking. At least, he did a good deal of worrying.

Work closely with Thorr, Gus Peavey had said. Listen to him but keep a checkrein on him. You can't dominate the son of a bitch, so give up that idea. Use a little tact. Get him to cooperate with you . . . .

Mr. Sample had, in his opinion, been veritably smothering the man with tact for some time now, with no improvement in their relationship. However, after a full day of dusty meditation, his only conclusion was that he must keep trying.

"Whether we like it or not, we're in this together," he said to Thorr that evening. He had washed off some of the dust in his hotel room and washed down some of it with a quick drink at the Star Bucket saloon, and he and Thorr were seated across Thorr's desk from each other.

Thorr gave him a flat look that seemed to indicate he didn't consider the remark worth a reply. Sample went on boldly.

"We should have guessed that Mrs. Farnum was planning to extend to Star City."

"Who knows what a woman's going to do?" Thorr said.

"We have to do something right away, Jack."

"I already did. I might have made a mistake."

"A — mistake?"

"I figured if we could break her down on the first trip, we'd make a monkey out of her," Thorr said. "I sent a couple boys out to hit her first swing station. They was supposed to be back here at noon. They ain't back. Her coach from Star rolled in almost two hours ago. Ours is two hours overdue and no sign of it.''

Sample took a moment to digest that and to remind himself to be tactful. ''You think something went wrong?''

Thorr gave him his flat look again. Then he said, ''You're goddamn right something went wrong. Asa Maidenlane is here.''

Sample knew the name well enough. He tried to keep his voice even. ''She hired a gunfighter?''

''He went out on the box this morning and he come back on the box tonight.''

''Well. I suppose — I mean you don't know if he —''

''I don't know nothing,'' Thorr said. ''An hour ago I sent Carter Hanford out to find out where the southbound is at and where my boys is at. They could be dead.''

''Well. I guess there's nothing to do but wait.'' Sample stared at the desktop thoughtfully. He tried to think of something cheerful. ''Mrs. Farnum is overextended, I'm sure. Financially and every other way. What do you make of that senseless road she's building into the Lost Tribes?''

''Nothing.''

''There have been no new mineral deposits discovered there, far as I can find out — no mines opening up or anything like that. Do you think — ''

''We got to get rid of Maidenlane, Mr. Sample.''

''You're probably right, but let's think it out. If we knew what the Farnum woman is up to, then we'd know what to do.''

''He won't buy off and he won't scare off.''

''Sounds like you know him,'' Sample said.

''Back a ways.''

Thorr was worried, Sample realized, and some of his

57

truculence was gone. Sample had not seen him in this mood before.

"Peavey don't want nobody hurt," Thorr complained, "unless it looks like an accident."

"There are good reasons for that. I'm sure you understand. He'll eventually force the Farnum woman out of business, but he has competition elsewhere." Sample tried a small smile. "An accident. Maybe we can work something out."

There were voices in the outer office. The clerk sounded excited. Only a few words were distinct, but it was clear that he was trying to keep someone from coming in to see Thorr. Thorr reached under his coat and got hold of the big short-barreled revolver he carried in a shoulder holster.

The door opened. The clerk peeked around it and was pushed aside, and Asa Maidenlane came in.

"Hello, Jack."

Thorr kept his hand on the revolver without drawing it. Maidenlane kicked the door shut, hands on hips, right fingers almost touching the butt of his low-slung gun.

"You going to pull it, Jack?" he said. "We can close the book right now."

Thorr slowly withdrew his hand. "Hello, Ace."

Maidenlane considered Sample, who had got to his feet and stepped to one side.

"You're Peavey's lawyer?"

"I represent Peavey & Company in certain matters, yes."

Maidenlane unfolded a paper and placed it on the desk in front of Thorr.

"We used twelve of your horses today, Jack. One team is in our barn here in town. You can send somebody over for it. We'll keep the other team as payment for Oc

Buckley's barn and saddle horse your boys shot. That's a bill of sale for you to sign."

Sample snatched up the paper and thrust it toward Maidenlane. "You're out of your mind, mister."

Maidenlane ignored him and spoke to Thorr. "We can go to court over this, Jack, if you'd rather."

"Of course, we'll go to court," Sample said. "If you helped yourself to those horses, if that's why our stage is late, we'll nail you to a door."

Thorr rose, snatched the bill of sale from Sample and sat down again, squinting at it.

"We've got your boys dead to rights," Maidenlane said. "Arson. Horse stealing. They'll be facing a heavy sentence. They might be persuaded to talk — a whole lot."

"I know a bluff when I see one," Sample said.

Thorr laid the bill of sale on the desk, smoothing it with his fingers. He reached for an inkstand and pulled it close.

"Don't sign it!" Sample snapped.

Thorr picked up a pen, dipped it in the inkwell.

"At least wait till we know exactly what happened," Sample pleaded.

Thorr didn't even look up at him. He scratched a signature and shoved the document toward Maidenlane.

"I don't understand you," Sample said. "You let this man bluff you."

"I made a mistake," Thorr said. "I'll pay for it. You leave me and Ace alone now."

Sample stared from one man to the other. Then he sighed mightily, whirled and left the room.

Maidenlane folded the bill of sale and tucked it into his shirt pocket. He dropped into the vacant chair across the desk from Thorr. Thorr nodded at the door through which Sample had disappeared.

59

"Was he right? You bluffing?"

"No," Maidenlane said.

"Where's my boys?"

"Finchleen station. They weren't up to the ride home."

"Bad hurt?"

"A kid stomped 'em some."

"A kid?" Thorr gave a small show of surprise.

"I had a gun on them."

Thorr gave a little twist of his head. "I doubt you could scare those two into talking much."

"Then why did you sign a bill of sale?"

Thorr nodded toward the door again. "That little bastard. He's got the law sewed up here. A trial would likely make him look good. It would be a lot of bother for me. . . . Besides, you and me ought to play this out our way."

"The last hand, Jack?"

"For one of us. You see Dolly?"

"Dolly is here?"

"You didn't know?" Thorr said. "I figured maybe she was what brought you."

"No."

"What then?"

"A job," Maidenlane said.

"You going to see Dolly?"

"No reason why I should."

"No," Thorr said, perhaps too quickly.

They sat in silence, despising each other and yet for this moment brothers of a sort in the sharing of old and festered hatred that might kill them both. Maidenlane rose and moved to the door and left the office, somehow casual about it, although he never once put his back to the other man.

"The last hand," Thorr said, wishing for a drink.

9

THE FARNUM EASTBOUND for Devil's Claw was an hour out of Augsburg and the day was already beginning to get hot. Pete Lafortune rode backward in the forward seat of the crowded coach, his laced, knee-high engineer's boots dovetailed between the lower extremities of a wary-eyed spinster and those of a talkative farm wife who was on her way to oversee the birth of a grandchild, had been up half the night canning peaches, believed in wider application of the Dawes Act, suffered from what she called "twitchity sciatica" and had a brother-in-law who had ridden an electric streetcar in Baltimore.

Pete slouched down in his seat as best he could without violating the proprieties of dovetailing, tipped his hat over his eyes and prepared to catch up on sleep — which he had been short of ever since undertaking to build a road over unknown terrain, in record time, at minimum cost and with a river crossing he had never seen but that would have to be ferried. It was the kind of drive-ahead, beat-the-devil project that Pete liked, however. Having got crews at work on this side of the range, he was now eager to get to the other and figure out where in tarnation they were headed.

He was just dozing off when the coach skidded, careened crazily and overturned in an explosion of screams, curses and splintering wood. Pete surfaced in a tangle of legs and petticoats. He got a door open, pulled himself out and began to extricate others. As he lifted the spinster clear of the coach, she was also somehow cleared of skirts and emerged in pink pantaloons trimmed with white lace. When she became aware of this, she tried to climb back through the stage door and he had to push her away. Finally she minced around to the far side of the coach and stood peeking over it until the others were out.

The driver, who had jumped clear, was having a bad time with the horses. Half of them were down, struggling in tangled harness, and the others were plunging and rearing. Pete grabbed the bit of one of the wheelers and got him quieted. The driver untangled the others and got two of them on their feet. The third, one of the little pointers, had a broken leg.

One of the male passengers was looking forlornly at a handful of crushed cigars. Another was trying to get some shape into a crushed derby. Other passengers were taking inventory of scratches and bruises, rips and tears. The garrulous farm wife had bit her lip in midsentence and was sitting on a suitcase, spitting blood. The spinster's lacey backside put Pete in mind of a birthday cake ludicrously balanced on the coach door as she rummaged inside for her lost garments. Miraculously, no one seemed to be seriously hurt.

Pete walked over to a clump of uprooted sage beside the road. He picked it up to display a length of baling wire attached to it.

"Trip wire," the driver said. "By God, the Peavey coach isn't more than half an hour ahead. That had to be strung within the last few minutes."

They looked into the distance then, and they both saw him, a rider watching from the top of a rise half a mile away. Even as they glimpsed him, he swung his horse and disappeared over the crest.

"Too far off to recognize," the driver said, "but I'll bet a gold watch against a buttonhook that was Ike McCabe."

"Who's he?" Pete asked.

"Keeps the first Peavey station on this run. He used to

keep station for Jim Farnum, but he went over to Peavey. Farnum fired his hay, now he's hitting back. At least, that's the talk. We've had wheel nuts loosened, felloes sawed through, brake shoes greased and God knows what-all.''

"Sheriff's not much help?''

"Haller?'' The driver snorted. "He stomps around and acts mad and swears he'll get the bastard if it's the last thing he does. Then he goes into the saloon and plays cards.''

Pete spotted a line of hoofprints a few yards away. He went over and hunkered down to study them. The driver hunkered down beside him.

"Seems like he was foolish not to stay on the road,'' Pete said.

"Probably has some idea of putting down a false trail,'' the driver said. "He rode off west, wants us to think he's headed for Augsburg. Chances are he'll wind around a bit, circle back to the road after a while and ride east.''

Pete scanned each hoofprint, fixing the pattern of the shoe in mind. One front shoe was fairly well worn, the other was brand new. The rear shoes were both calked.

The male passengers heaved the coach upright. One door was off its hinges. One wheel was wobbly. The railing on top of the coach was bent and broken on the right side. Inside, the center seat had torn loose from the floor.

The driver shot the horse with the broken leg on the spot. Two other horses were too lame to go on. A third had a bad shoulder bruise. Harness was tangled and broken.

The driver mounted one of the sound animals and rode off toward Augsburg, assuring the passengers he'd be back with a new coach and hitch. Pete got aboard the other uninjured animal, a big wheeler, and set out in the opposite direction.

63

After a half-hour, crotch-splitting ride, he reached McCabe station and turned in. Mrs. McCabe opened the door and stood peeking around it as he climbed the porch steps. She was a bright-eyed woman, still slender and pretty after a decade and a half of child bearing. She looked uneasy as Pete told her about the accident, even though he didn't mention the tripwire. He pretended to be looking for the Farnum station and to have turned in here by mistake. She gave him curt directions, still shielded by the partly open door.

Pete was half French and half Irish. He turned on his best combination of chivalry and blarney, got her into a chatty mood, and soon she stepped out on the porch, jabbering away about the time she had been to Kansas City. This had been when she was a child, it turned out, but it was the great adventure of her life, and Pete kept her talking for a quarter of an hour.

Ike McCabe rode into the yard then. He glanced at Pete and at the big coach horse tied to the hitchrail and rode directly to the barn. Pete apologized to Mrs. McCabe for taking so much of her time. He went down the steps and past the hitchrail for a look at the tracks left by McCabe's horse. The near front shoe was new. The hind shoes were calked.

McCabe came out of the barn, meeting Pete as he returned to the hitchrail.

"What you want here, mister?"

"Looking for the Farnum station," Pete said. "The stage piled up about eight miles back."

"That so? Anybody hurt bad?"

"I don't think so," Pete said.

McCabe was lean, muscular, long-faced. There was an air of pious hostility about him. He tipped his chin at Pete and regarded him narrowly. "You work for Farnum. You're the engineer."

"Yes, sir."

"You're building a road. Folks are wondering where it's going."

Pete laughed. "Sometimes I wonder, too."

McCabe was not amused. "You ain't going to tell me?"

"I'm surprised you haven't guessed."

Mrs. McCabe called down from the porch. "Man's lost, Ike. He came to the wrong station."

"He ain't lost," McCabe said.

Pete considered the problem of getting on the big wheel horse without stirrups. He considered asking McCabe for a boost and decided not to. He led the horse close to the porch steps and made the ascent. He tipped his hat to Mrs. McCabe and left.

April was dozing in a chair, waiting for word on the Augsburg coach, when Link knocked on her door and reported that it had finally arrived, three hours late. Asa Maidenlane and Pete Lafortune were with him, and they all came into the parlor.

Pete told about identifying the tracks of McCabe's horse. "It's evidence a trial lawyer could shoot full of holes," he said, "but as far as I'm concerned, it's conclusive."

"A hundred percent," Link agreed, turning to Maidenlane. "McCabe is in your department now, Ace."

Maidenlane accepted that with a nod. April frowned.

"I've always liked Irene McCabe," she said. "And Ike is more fool than anything else."

"A dangerous fool," Pete said.

"What will you do, Ace?" April asked.

"He can get out of the territory or go to guns."

"He's stubborn enough to fight," she said.

"His choice."

" No, there has to be a better — a kinder way," she said thoughtfully.

"Kinder?" Link Arbuckle said.

"He hardly deserves kindness, but his wife and children do. Don't cringe, gentlemen, but I think I'm getting an idea. You leave Ike McCabe to me."

10

THEY MET AT the ranch for breakfast — April, Link,
Tom Lawrence, Maidenlane and Pete Lafortune. April
went into a bedroom and changed into a pair of Jim's jeans
that Sally Smithwick, disapproving and protesting, had
cut down for her. The men made no comment but were
obviously ill at ease as they sat down to breakfast.

They considered that she was out of her mind, she
supposed. For a female to wear pants was considered —
well, to put it mildly, vulgar, and to ride astride, obscene.

"I don't care!" she said suddenly. "We have a river to
swim the horses across. I am not going to undertake that
sitting sidesaddle in five pounds of flowing riding skirt!"

"Under the circumstances," Tom Lawrence said,
"your costume is sensible and appropriate."

"Cute, too," Asa Maidenlane said.

"What?"

"Cute."

"I have no desire to look *cute*," she exploded. "I have
a business to run, a shortcut to build, and — God damn it
to hell! There. I'm surrounded by men; I might as well talk
like one, too."

They laughed at that, and the strain was eased.

"You've decided to accept me?"

"What choice do we have?" Maidenlane said.

She started to glare at him, but the others laughed again
and she joined in.

"Of course we accept you," Tom Lawrence said.

His ingratiating tone annoyed her. "I suppose if I were
ten feet tall and had a green nose, you'd accept me, too."

"Absolutely."

Men, she thought. They can dig themselves into a hole and not even know it. She met Maidenlane's eyes and saw understanding and amusement in them, amusement that for a fleeting moment she shared. She was on the edge of a thought that she swept aside. He's a monster, she told herself, a perceptive man who is also a killer.

A few minutes later, the five of them rode out of the ranch gate and cantered across the stage road. They reached the first easy slope of the Lost Tribes and slowed to a walk as they began to climb. The grade grew steeper; they wound their way up to a summit, then to another and another. The river lay far below them, a jeweled bottom to the slender, high-walled gorge that cleft this range. They turned north, following the crest of this eastern shoulder. There was no trail. Sometimes the bend of the land took them away from the rim of the gorge, sometimes they rode close to it. Looking down, they saw that the river filled the gorge wall to wall; rarely was there a skimpy rind of beach. When there was, the wall rose precipitously above it, often sheer and richly colored, sometimes scaled with ledges and niches where vegetation struggled bravely for a roothold.

After a few miles, the little party descended a slope to a timber-spotted saddle that fell away on its west side into a ravine. Surprisingly, this led downward to the river at a place where the bank was only a few feet high. April reined up and dismounted.

"Stretch our legs," she said.

The men slid out of their saddles and walked to the edge of the bank. There was a tiny lip of beach below it and a game trail down. The river was about fifty yards wide. It looked deep, and the current swift enough to be treacherous. Pete Lafortune scowled at the high ragged wall across the water from them. He looked upstream, then own. He shook his head in bewilderment.

"Where do we cross?"

"Right here," April said.

The men looked at her as if she must be joking. She waited smugly till Pete voiced the obvious objection.

"Where in tarnation do we go ashore?"

"Look again."

They looked. Across the river the face of the gorge was seamed, stratified, ragged, but it was perpendicular, and the river flowed deep against it. A big slab rose out of the water, a blunted rock triangle that came to an apex sixty feet above the river.

"Look closely," April said. "Study that slab."

They studied. Asa Maidenlane jounced down the short trail to the beach. He took off his hat and held it at arm's length as a shield against reflected sunlight. The others followed him down.

"It's sort of an optical illusion," April said.

The slab seemed part of the cliff face, boldly sculptured in deep relief. This impression was reinforced by an eddy where the current bit into the upstream edge of the slab and swirled frothily back into the mainstream. But on the downstream side a long convex line curved down the cliff and ended near the top of the slab or — if one looked closely — ran behind it.

"The slab is separate from the wall on the downstream side," Maidenlane said. "Is there a beach behind it?"

"Bigger than you'd think," April said.

They stared for a moment. Then Pete Lafortune said, "I'll take your word for it. But where do we go from the beach?"

"Look where I'm pointing," April said. "See that line above the slab? It looks like a seam in the cliff, but it isn't. What looks from here like solid wall is really two overlap-

ping sections of wall, one a little behind the other. There's
a passage in between. The slab hides it. Come on. You'll
see.''

They led the horses down to the beach. They took off
their boots, then the men took off their shirts.

"You'd better do the same," Maidenlane told her. "If
you have to swim, wet sleeves will do you in quick."

"It really doesn't matter," she said. "I can't swim
anyway."

She led the way. There was a quick drop-off from the
beach, and the horses were quickly swimming. Riders
kicked free of stirrups and clung to saddlehorns. The
current was strong, though not raging. The danger was
that the horses would be carried below the landing place
and trapped between towering walls with no place to get
ashore; so it was necessary to keep them angled upstream.
The animals, not seeing a landing place anyway, resisted
this and were difficult to guide.

A few yards short of the slab they got their feet under
them, and it was easy to work them around the south edge
and across a shallow backwater to a surprisingly large
beach.

It could be seen now how, partly hidden by the slab, a
winding break in the cliff wall was all but impossible to
make out from the far bank. The slab projected from the
north section of wall and marked the end of that section.
The south section tapered off inland and ended abruptly
behind the slab in a towering point. This promontory
wasn't noticeable above the slab because of still another
cliff that bent around from the north to run behind it and
blend with it visually.

There was a space of eight or ten yards between, however, as the riders discovered when they hairpinned
around the point. They were in a deep, pinched little

canyon — hardly more than a crevasse. They followed this on a winding course for a quarter of a mile, climbing gently and then turning suddenly into a long gulch.

A stand of thick timber grew at the mouth of the narrow passage, effectively hiding it. The eastern slope of the gulch was also mottled with timber. The western, steep and rocky, was barren except for scraggly jack pine and juniper. Uncomfortable in wet clothes and saddles, the party followed the gulch floor for a short distance; then they climbed to the summit of the eastern slope and turned south, riding above the river again before turning west along a hogback. They struck a trail, followed it up a slow-pitched grade and were at the crest of the Lost Tribes.

A little way down the western slope, they ran into Pete's surveying crew. Farther along, they reached his advance camp and paused to stretch their legs.

Pete was exuberant. "You could almost get a coach over our back trail right now, except for the river. The ferry's going to be a bit of a problem, but we'll figure out something."

"A problem? Why?" April said sharply, a challenge in her voice that she immediately regretted. "I don't expect anything fancy — just a big raft on a cable with a mule team to pull it back and forth."

They were standing around a chuck wagon. The cook, the only man in camp, was pouring coffee into tin cups. April accepted one, finding the coffee lukewarm and stale.

"We can do better than mules," Pete said. "I know of a steam engine I can get at a mine that shut down near Adako Falls."

"I suppose that would be neater," she said indecisively. She looked around for Maidenlane and saw that he had climbed up on a stump and was looking in the direction from which they had come.

"Altogether more satisfactory," Pete said. "Cheaper, too, at least in the long run. But the problem is a landing place on the west bank. We'll have to build a dock, and there's no way to do it with that slab there. We're going to have to blast it away, which will be tricky and dangerous. God knows what kind of debris we'll bring down from those cliffs."

Tom Lawrence and Link were standing by, sipping coffee, listening. Link, a quiet man usually slow to disagree, said that he didn't see why blasting was necessary, and he put forth a plan to fill in the backwater behind the slab and build a dock against the cliff to the south. Pete had to admit the idea had merit, and the two fell into a discussion about it.

April watched Maidenlane, who had climbed down from the stump and was mounting his horse. He reined up the back trail and disappeared into a patch of timber above the camp. After a moment, he reappeared. He rode back to camp at a trot and swung down from the saddle.

"Man's been trailing us," he said. "He turned back when he saw me, but I got a good look at him. Small man in a dark suit. Carries a shotgun."

"Carter Hanford," Link said. "Thorr's office guard."

Maidenlane nodded, frowning. "I expect so."

"So Thorr will know what we're up to," Tom Lawrence said. "I can't see that it matters much."

"It doesn't," April said. "We couldn't have kept it a secret much longer anyway. Pete, how long will it take?"

"The road's easy. I'll have it finished in three weeks," Pete said. "The ferry may take a bit longer, not much. That's provided I can hire all the men I want — and provided the weather holds."

He scowled across the ragged tableland below them and pointed to a darkness in the sky to the west. "We can expect a storm or two this time of year, I suppose."

Maidenlane turned to stare thoughtfully up the back trail again. "Carter Hanford," he said. "I don't know the man, but I've heard the name. He was a sidekick of Jase and Bucky Rome."

Rome. April struggled with memory to put meaning to the name. The Rome brothers. Asa Maidenlane had brought them in. When they had mounted up and were on their way down the western slope, she fell back beside Link and asked what had happened to the Romes.

"They stood trial at Bismarck," Link said. "They were both hanged."

11

CARTER HANFORD SLOUCHED in his chair beside Thorr's desk, hands in pockets, shotgun on the floor beside him. His eyes were fixed unwaveringly on a point above the head of Mr. Sample, who stood before the desk, hands behind his back.

"Why," Sample asked Jack Thorr, "is she going to the expense of building a short route that we can use, too?"

Thorr brought his hand down on the desk in a chopping motion. "She must figure to cut us off at the crossing."

Sample turned on Hanford, glaring. "Would you say a bridge could be built at that crossing?"

Hanford took his hands out of his pockets and straightened in his chair. He threw a questioning look at Thorr.

"Mr. Sample talks to everybody like they was on the witness stand," Thorr said.

"It would take a right fancy bridge," Hanford said.

"A ferry would be more likely," Thorr said.

"A toll ferry!" Sample said.

"That's the way I unriddle it," Thorr said.

"But she can't — not without permission from the legislature. Good heavens, you don't suppose she's got it?"

"I don't suppose nothing," Thorr said.

"Good Lord! Her lawyer was in Helena just before the legislature adjourned. We should have found out what he was up to."

"Not 'we,' " Thorr said. "Things like that is up to Gus Peavey's high-priced lawyers."

Carter Hanford allowed himself one restrained snort of laughter. Sample reminded himself to be tactful and produced a compressed smile.

"You're right, Jack. Mr. Peavey has a man who's supposed to keep his eye on the legislature. Well, at least we know what that road means now. You've done a good job, both of you."

Thorr gave him his flat look. Carter Hanford stared upward. Sample assured himself that they really appreciated his approval; they simply didn't know how to respond gracefully.

"Well, boys, I've got work to do," he said cheerfully. "I'll say good night."

When the door had closed on him, Thorr said mildly, "You see what I'm up against?"

"You can hear his brains slosh," Hanford said.

"He was in a hurry to get out of here. You know why? He's going to write a report about what you found out. He's going to get it off to old Gus in the morning mail. What he don't know is, I sent a messenger horseback three hours ago."

Hanford laughed, three snorts this time. "Little pissant."

"He's useful in some ways, if he'd stay in his own backyard. He's stoppled off the Farnum woman's credit, only I don't think she knows it yet. She's going to be hard put to meet her payroll for that road crew."

Hanford glanced down at the shotgun on the floor beside him. "I could have had Maidenlane today, Jack. When he spotted me, he rode back for a closer look, right into a patch of timber. I could have set myself behind a tree and blowed him out of the saddle."

"Good thing you didn't."

"I know. Any killing has got to look like an accident. I'll tell you honest, though. I'd have done it today except for one thing. There was a surveying crew a little ways above that camp. They'd got a good look at me."

"You listen here, Carter. Don't go off at half-cock now, for Christ sake. The time has got to be just right."

"I get to thinking about the Rome boys. I was like a third brother, Jack. Now the bastard that brought 'em in is here right under my nose. Seems providential."

"I want him as bad as you do, Carter."

"Then listen to this. The Farnum outfit is onto McCabe, I figure. Maidenlane is on that side of the range. I figure he'll pay McCabe a visit, maybe to kill him, maybe just to put the fear of God into him. Suppose I happen to be at McCabe station when he comes in. Suppose he gets his head blowed off."

Thorr considered this with a sudden narrow interest. "Inside the station?"

"Suppose the McCabes swear he come in gun in hand. Suppose there's been a shot fired from his gun. Nobody could say that I was there gunning for him. They'll say he went there to kill McCabe and got unlucky."

Thorr indulged in a small and thoughtful nod, then he frowned. "You'll have to get rid of the McCabe kids some way."

"They could be sent out of the house when we see him coming."

"You figure he'll drop in there tomorrow?"

"Seems worth looking into, that's all."

"You'd have to ride all night. Unlessen you take the new shortcut."

"I'll go the long way. I don't take to swimming that river in the dark."

A low rumble of thunder sounded distantly and rolled

76

closer, rattling the window. The two men listened gravely.

"Looks like you'll get your ass wet anyway," Thorr said.

"I got a poncho."

"Now listen to me," Thorr said. "It's got to happen just like you laid it out. At McCabe's place. You got to plan it with the McCabes so they'll swear he come in shooting. If it don't work out just exactly, then you got to call it off."

"I'll get started right now."

When Hanford had left, Thorr sat still for a long time. It was a good plan. Ike McCabe wouldn't take any prizes for likableness, but his wife was well thought of. If Maidenlane went gunning for Ike and got killed, nobody would say it was Peavey & Company that was doing the dirty. If Carter did this right, he was likely to come out of it more a hero than anything else.

There was another long roll of thunder, starting soft and growing loud like the last. Thunder usually didn't sound like that, Thorr thought. You expected it to come on loud and then roll away in the distance. An Indian would say that this thunder was some sort of sign — whether good or bad, Thorr didn't know.

The storm struck noisily and hard, slashing the mountains, soaking the thirsty flatland. Chain lightning devil-danced on the Lost Tribe buttes. Wind pressed rain into sheets, twisted it into torrents.

Carter Hanford, hat pulled low — man, saddle and shotgun cocooned in a great poncho — saw no mystical significance in bad weather. His concern was that it might delay his journey or, if it lasted through the next day, keep Maidenlane away from McCabe station. He stopped three

77

times during the night, getting stationkeepers out of bed, demanding fresh horses, refusing refreshment and pressing on quickly.

Dismal daylight was creeping into the world when he reached McCabe's. The rain had stopped, leaving the road a river of mud and the station yard a marsh. He slogged his horse across it and left the animal at the hitchrail. Poncho dripping, he climbed the stairs to the porch and swept into the station like some winged reptilian creature out of Dante, washed up from the netherworld during the night.

The McCabes were at breakfast, all seven of them. Even they, somewhat inured to traveling apparitions, were startled. Mrs. McCabe gasped a perfunctory welcome. Then, as Hanford emerged from his India rubber shroud, Ike McCabe saw the shotgun and recognized the man.

"Mr. Hanford." McCabe got to his feet.

Hanford responded with a sharp nod. He took off his derby and slapped water on the floor. McCabe made an effort at cheeriness.

"If ever I saw a man in need of hot coffee, you're it."

"Obliged," Hanford said. "And I got a horse needs tending. Asa Maidenlane been to see you?"

"Me?"

"You. He didn't come yesterday?"

"No, sir. What would he want with me?"

"Skedaddle the kids. I'll talk private to you and the missus."

The two McCabe boys, who looked about twelve and fourteen, were sent to stable Hanford's horse. Two girls, younger, were sent to make beds. The third girl, hardly more than a toddler, went with them. Hanford sat down at the table and swallowed a gulp of the coffee Mrs. McCabe set before him.

"Maidenlane is on this side of the mountains. It's only a hunch, but we figure he might come down on you. He's a deadly man."

"What does he want with Ike?" Mrs. McCabe said.

Hanford sipped his coffee. He looked from one to the other and let the silence hang.

"She don't know," McCabe said.

"You better tell her."

McCabe shifted uneasily in his chair. "I been doing special work for Thorr."

"I suspicioned it," Mrs. McCabe said.

"Dangerous work," Hanford said.

"But they wouldn't send a gunman after him!" Mrs. McCabe protested. "April Farnum wouldn't do that."

"Well, ma'am, my hunch might be wrong. But I'll spend a day or two with you, just in case."

"Appreciate that," McCabe said.

"Maidenlane is a rattlesnake," Hanford said. "He'll talk pleasant to you one second, and the next his gun will be in his hand and you'll be dead. So we'll take no chances with him. I want you to keep the back door locked. I want a table put directly in front of the front door. I'll be setting there when he comes in."

Mrs. McCabe frowned. "What if he comes peaceful?"

"Ma'am, if he comes here, it will be for just one thing. Let's say it flat out. It will be to kill your husband."

She turned to McCabe, her eyes big in a face the color of a wrung-out dishrag.

"It will be all right," McCabe said. "We'll do as Mr. Hanford says."

Hanford ate a hearty breakfast, giving instruction between bites. Then he and McCabe positioned a table opposite the front door. Hanford sat down behind it, shotgun on the table beside him. He sat with the door partly open so he could watch the yard. Mrs. McCabe offered to bring him another cup of coffee, but he refused it.

"I'll just wait," he said.

"You ought to get a little sleep," McCabe said. "I'll keep watch."

"I'll just wait."

He stretched his legs when the eastbound coach arrived, watching through one of the windows that flanked the door as McCabe and his boys changed teams, and passengers sloshed through mud to the privy. After the stage had gone on, McCabe came inside, leaving the boys busy at chores in the barn. The girls played quietly with dolls in a far corner of the station.

Mrs. McCabe had gone to the stove to fix a noon meal when Hanford made the announcement.

"Buggy coming into the yard."

McCabe went to the window to the left of the door. "Two people in it. One of 'em's a woman."

Hanford had gone to the door and was peering around it. "It's him. God Almighty, the Farnum woman is with him."

"He must have come peaceful," McCabe said uncertainly.

"He's a sly one," Hanford said. "If he comes in alone, we'll do it just like I said. Skedaddle those kids."

He closed the door and went back to the table and sat down.

12

AUGSBURG WAS THE county seat. For weeks now rumors had swept it like the flocks of English sparrows that roosted under its eaves and subsisted on its horse manure. A new mine would start operations in the Lost Tribes, and April Farnum was building a road to the site. A new mine would *not* start operations in the Lost Tribes. April Farnum had found a shortcut to Devil's Claw. April Farnum had *not* found a shortcut to Devil's Claw. Somebody had honeyfuggled her into building a road to nowhere, and she was crazy in the head. Rumors, fantasies, jokes, gossip. When the Farnum company manager, its lawyer, an engineer, and a gunfighter jogged into town accompanied by April herself, wearing pants and sitting a man's saddle, a new brood flew the streets.

"Whatever you're up to, it's clearly a preposterous gamble," Bartholomew Smith, president of the Rocky Mountain Bank & Trust Company, said when April, Tom Lawrence, and Link were seated in his office at the rear of the long stone building that housed the bank. He smiled when he said it.

The bank had a branch in Devil's Claw, but the Farnum company had always dealt directly with its president on matters other than routine. Bart Smith understood the financial position of the company and more than once had come up with a crucial loan without red tape or delay. He was, April thought, as close to an old friend as it's possible for a banker to be.

She and the others had got into Augsburg just after noon and had taken rooms at the hotel. She had brushed the wrinkles from a simple serge suit that she had crammed into saddlebags, and she was now a lady again.

"Hardly preposterous, Bart," she said. "There's a way to cross the Lost Tribes, and we're building a shortcut over it."

"We came over it this morning," Tom Lawrence said. "What's more, the Farnum company will have a degree of control over it."

Tom went on to explain about the river crossing. He produced a certified copy of the paragraph in the bill that granted April the right to operate a toll ferry.

Bart Smith was a youngish, almost painfully handsome man with gray-black hair, dark eyes, a sharp-cut nose. He put on a pair of spectacles, glanced quickly at the paper and handed it back. Removing the spectacles, he gave April a puzzled look.

"You're really declaring war, aren't you?"

"Good Lord, Bart. Jim's dead. How can you say *I'm* declaring war?"

"You're committing funds in a big way."

"I'm building twenty miles of road and a ferry," April said. "Pete Lafortune estimates that only about a third of the road will need to be graded. He wants to corduroy a few low places, and that's it. He says he'll finish it in less than a month, using thirty men and twelve teams. We pay two dollars a day for labor, four dollars for a man who brings his own team. Plus hay and beans, of course. We have men and horses on the ranch that will do the road work east of the river. Some of them will also work on the ferry. We'll need another ten men for a week to cut logs for the ferry. We'll need a steam engine and some cable. The whole project won't cost over five thousand dollars. I want to borrow thirty-five hundred, Bart."

Smith squinted painfully. He made a helpless gesture. "Absolutely not, April. I'm sorry."

"Bart, we've borrowed off and on from you for years. We have no outstanding debt. What do you mean?"

"This is different," Smith said. "You're getting into an expensive war with Peavey & Company. This bank isn't going to get involved. We're not going to take the first step, April."

"Bart," Link Arbuckle said, "this bank was just a safe in the back room of your father-in-law's store until Jim Farnum brought his stage line through."

"I won't argue that," Smith said, "but there were other factors in our growth, too, including our own prudent judgment. You can't beat Peavey & Company, April. You're not anywhere near rich enough. If Peavey can't use your ferry, they'll take it by force and fight you in court. They'll hire a dozen lawyers. They'll buy judges."

"And bankers," Tom Lawrence said. "It looks to me like they've already started."

Smith made his helpless gesture again. "They're putting pressure on us, I don't deny it. They've forced us to choose sides. Can you fault a banker for choosing the stronger?"

April got to her feet and the others did, too. "I'm sorry," Bartholomew Smith said again as she opened the door.

When they were on the boardwalk on their way back to the hotel, April said, "It's all right. I have some personal funds. I'll draw on the ranch account. I'll raise what we need somehow."

She clutched at her hair as the wind tore at it. Street dust spiraled into plumes and slapped into their faces. The sun slid in and out of fast moving clouds.

"I've got about a thousand stashed away," Link said. "Count it in."

"No, Link. Thanks, but I won't do that."

"The offer isn't entirely unselfish. I've got a job to protect."

"No," she said. "It will be inconvenient, but I can raise the money to meet our payroll for the road. Then—"

Another gust stole her words. They walked on in silence, heads bowed against the wind. The hotel was set in a big rectangle of well-kept lawn, a three-story, white clapboard building with a porch all the way around it. Asa Maidenlane lounged in a rocking chair with his feet on the porch rail. April had asked him to meet her here and accompany her to McCabe station. They had passed the station on their way into town, but she hadn't felt up to a crucial confrontation with the McCabes then; it would have been bad strategy to approach them wearing pants.

Maidenlane got to his feet. "There's a buggy waiting at Hamm's barn," he said, dragging a big Raymond railroad watch out of his pocket and snapping open its hunting case. "But it's late now. After three."

"And it's going to rain," April said, not pausing on her way into the hotel. "We'll see the McCabes tomorrow."

She went upstairs to her room, sinking down on the bed, wanting to cry and telling herself that would be childish. She took off her shoes and stretched out on her back, bone-tired but too angry to sleep. She studied the rough, whitewashed boards of the ceiling, trying not to think. After a while she got up, undid her hair, and began to brush it, growing angrier with every stroke.

She would start her own bank, she thought. Why not? After she had beaten Peavey & Company or sold out to them at her price, she would take on the Rocky Mountain Bank & Trust Company. She would drive Bart Smith right out of the county. She would make Tom Lawrence president of her bank. Tom? Good Lord, no. Tom would lend money to every Patron of Husbandry, Knight of Labor, and Fourierist with a crusading gleam in his eye. And to every tickle-grass ne'er-do-well with a tear in his eye.

She laughed out loud, thinking that she was furious with Bart Smith for acting just as she might act if she were in his shoes. If a bank president had to choose, Peavey & Company was a far better bet than Farnum. She laughed again. It was better than crying.

There was a knock on the door. She got up and jerked it open, not caring that her hair was down. Asa Maidenlane was there, hat in hand, an unformed smile behind his eyes.

"Disturbing you?"

"I was brushing my hair."

"I heard somebody laugh. You don't have company?"

"I'm just quietly having hysterics," she said. "Come on in."

He stepped into the room. She closed the door. She turned to the mirror over the washstand and began to pin up her hair.

"I heard what happened at the bank," he said.

"Oh? You came to console me?"

"Thought you might like to talk."

"About what?"

"Thought you might be upset."

"Of course I'm upset!" She took a deep breath and forced herself to speak calmly. "I don't expect to die of it. Raising money is going to mean a lot of fuss and inconvenience I didn't expect, but I can do it."

He stood behind her, watching her face in the mirror. It was on the tip of her tongue to tell him he had a nerve barging in on her like this. He was hired to carry a gun, not to . . . She avoided his eyes.

"You're a woman to admire," he said.

He was standing close behind her. Unless I say exactly the right thing, he's going to touch me, she thought. If he

85

does, I must remember not to jump away violently but to put him in his place coldly, icily. Whatever I do, I mustn't scream. But now I must say exactly the right thing.

"Please," she said.

"You'll beat Peavey," he said. "Maybe your friends aren't as powerful as his, but they're devoted to you. Link, Tom Lawrence, that engineer. They'll go all the way for you."

"Please."

"Please what?"

"Please don't touch me."

Their eyes met in the mirror. Deliberately, his hands pressed her waist. Who did he think he was? Did he think he could barge in here and just take hold of her like this and —

She laid unused hairpins on the washstand and let her hair go. She turned, smiling, and raised her face to him.

After a long time she pushed away, whispering. She went to the door and threw the latch and came back to the strong-tender, hard-soft forgetfulness of his embrace.

"Please. Oh God, Ace, please."

Wind rattled the window, slashing dust against it. Thunder exploded dully and rolled closer.

13

THE RIDE TO McCabe station in the buggy took a bit more than two hours. The day was sweet after the rain. They flushed a covey of quail, startled an outraged rockchuck that reminded April of Oc Buckley, marveled that a tiger swallowtail had survived the stormy night. There were the wonders of talk and silence and laughter, the miracle of touch. The horse between the buggy shafts clowned and capered as if he caught their mood and was glad to be going somewhere in happy company. Ace had to hold him in at first to keep him from wearing himself out in the rubbery, rut-sliced mud.

Sometimes they teased each other. Sometimes they spoke with great earnestness. Sometimes they asked each other intimate questions, exploring boldly but with a certain formality.

"You could have charged me ten dollars a day," April said. "You asked three. You sort of insisted on it. Why?"

"A man makes his peace with himself," Ace said.

"You have to prove to yourself that you don't kill for money, is that it? You accept a living, no more."

"That's about it," he said.

She fell silent, frowning. Then she said suddenly, "That could amount to a terrible confession, couldn't it? You don't do it for money, so you do it because you like it."

"Like what?"

"What you do. Selling your gun. Killing."

"There are men who kill to get what they want. If nobody stood up to them, they'd own the world." He laughed then, dismissing profundity. "There. That takes care of my conscience."

April continued to frown. "You kill to stop the killers. And you like it."

"I like the risk, the game. Like it? Does a gambler like to gamble? He does it because he's uneasy when he's not gambling."

"Did you ever think of doing something else?"

"Often enough."

"Like what?"

He laughed again. "I could drive a stage."

"For a woman boss?"

"If she was pretty."

"And vulnerable?"

It was his turn to frown, not quite erasing his smile. "Vulnerable? Is that how you see it? I just happened to come along?"

"How else?" she said.

"If it hadn't been me...?"

"It happened to be you."

He was dissatisfied, displeased maybe. She could see that. He clucked needlessly at the horse. When he spoke it was of something else.

"You'll handle McCabe, you said. What are you going to do?"

"We'll have a talk. I want you there, too."

"I just sit there?"

"You'll be a great comfort," she said teasingly. She went on soberly. "I'm going to do a terrible thing to the McCabes. It isn't going to go down easily. You'll be there—you'll just *be* there—as a reminder that he'd better accept my terms."

They reached the station. It was in a low place to the right of the road. The barn was on a little rise fifty yards to the right of the house. The house was built high, with steps leading up to a porch across its front. The door was at the center of the porch with a mullioned window on each side of it. There was a hitchrail in front of the porch a few feet from the steps.

Maidenlane followed the ruts of the morning stage into the muddy yard, guiding the horse in a half circle past the barn and pulling up just short of the steps to the porch.

Three little girls appeared from in back of the house. They walked abreast, the older ones each holding a hand of the third, who was only three or four. They walked hesitantly in the mud, trying to hold their skirts high with their free hands, lifting the little one off the ground and swinging her forward.

"You go to the door," April said. "Ask Ike McCabe to come out. I want to talk to him alone—at least at first. I want to spare Irene McCabe all I can."

He handed her the reins but didn't get out of the buggy at once. He was watching the children. April leaned forward for a better view of them, wondering what interested him. They were headed toward the barn. After a few steps, they came to a stop as if despairing of making it through the mud. They did not look toward the buggy.

"You know their names?" Ace asked.

"Let's see. The fair-haired one, the oldest, is Jenny. The dark one is Louise."

He got down from the buggy, still watching them. He threw a glance at the porch and then waded through the mud toward the girls.

"Jenny!" he called.

Jenny picked up the little one and moved a few steps toward the barn. He overtook her, talking to her, asking questions that April couldn't hear clearly. He got shy, monosyllabic answers at first. Louise, who had hung

89

back, came up and joined them. Then both girls were talking more freely. April caught just a word or two. One of them, a name, stabbed her with a sudden fear.

"...shooed us out of the house...Mr. Hanford...in front of the door..."

Hanford? Carter Hanford here? She slid across the buggy seat as Ace sloshed back toward the steps. "Ace!" she hissed as he neared the buggy. "Let's get out of here."

He merely glanced at her as he walked past. He paused to scrape his boots on the bottom step. Then he took the steps two at a time. He strode along the porch, looking in the window to the right of the door as he passed.

The door was hinged on the right. He flung it open whirling to the left side of the doorway as the shotgun roared, the charge tearing away part of a support pos above the porch railing. Someone inside the house screamed. As Ace whirled, his Colt somehow was in his hand. His turn brought him to the window to the left of the door, and he fired through the glass, whirling again as a second blast sounded inside the house, doing no damage that April could see. There was another scream inside the house, and another.

Ace was at the door again, standing close to the jamb, peering cautiously around it. Then he stepped inside.

April found herself climbing down from the buggy. The little girls stood motionless in the mud, gaping at the house. Two boys came out of the barn and gaped. April stumbled up the steps, going over what she had seen, trying to comprehend it. The shooting had taken place in barely two seconds, too fast to grasp. She found herself talking out loud.

"He wasn't hit. He went inside. He's all right...."

TASTE 'EM!

KENT GOLDEN LIGHTS
ONLY 8 MG TAR
YET TASTES SO GOOD, YOU
WON'T BELIEVE THE NUMBERS.
(See other side for your brand's tar numbers.)

COMPARE YOUR NUMBERS TO KENT GOLDEN LIGHTS

FTC Report Dec. 1976

Filter Brands (Regulars)	MG TAR	MG NIC	Filter Brands (Menthols)	MG TAR	N
Kent Golden Lights* — King Size	**8**	**0.7**	**Kent Golden Lights* — Kings**	**8**	0
Lucky 100's — 100mm	9	0.6	Iceberg — 100mm	9	0
Pall Mall Extra Mild — King Size	10	0.7	Vantage — King Size	11	0
Vantage — King Size	10	0.7	Multifilter — King Size	11	0
Parliament* — King Size	10	0.7	Doral — King Size	11	0
Doral — King Size	13	0.9	Salem Lights — King Size	11	0
Multifilter — King Size	13	0.8	Fact — King Size	13	0
Marlboro Lights — King Size	13	0.8	Kool Milds — King Size	14	0
Winston Lights — King Size	13	0.9	Marlboro — King Size	14	0
Raleigh Extra Mild — King Size	14	1.0	Belair — King Size	15	1
Viceroy Extra Mild — King Size	14	1.0	Alpine — King Size	15	1
Fact — King Size	14	1.0	Virginia Slims — 100mm	16	0
Viceroy — King Size	16	1.0	Saratoga — 120mm	16	1
Virginia Slims — 100mm	16	0.9	Silva Thins — 100mm	16	1
L&M — 100mm	17	1.1	Pall Mall — 100mm	16	1
Benson & Hedges — 100mm	18	1.0	Eve — 100mm	17	1
Pall Mall — King Size	18	1.2	Kool — King Size	17	1
Lark — King Size	18	1.1	Benson & Hedges — 100mm	18	1
Marlboro — King Size	18	1.1	Salem — King Size	18	
Winston — King Size	19	1.2	Winston — 100mm	19	
Tareyton — King Size	20	1.3	More — 120mm	21	
Lowest of All Brands Sold	0.5	0.05	Lowest of All Brands Sold	0.5	

*FTC Method

*FTC Method

KENT GOLDEN LIGHTS ONLY 8 MG TAR

AS LOW AS YOU CAN GO AND STILL GET GOOD TASTE AND SMOKING SATISFACTION.

Kent Golden Lights Regular & Menthol: 8 mg. "tar," 0.7 mg. nicotine av. per cigarette by FTC Method.

Warning: The Surgeon General Has Determined That Cigarette Smoking Is Dangerous to Your Health.

He was standing beside a pine table directly in front of the doorway, dropping his gun into its holster. There was a big splash of blood on the tabletop. Ike McCabe was on one knee behind the table, turning Carter Hanford on his back. Irene McCabe, head bowed, clung to the back of a chair.

"Not quite gone yet," McCabe announced. "He's fading fast."

"Mrs. Farnum," Irene McCabe said weakly. She started toward April and then grabbed the chair again. "We couldn't help it. We had to do what he said. He come early this morning and he said..."

April didn't hear the rest of it. She moved close to Carter Hanford and had her look. The lower part of his face and his neck were covered solidly with blood. His mouth was open and seemed to be full of blood. His eyes were closed.

"Hit in the throat," Ike McCabe said.

April went back to the porch and leaned against the shot-torn post. Irene McCabe came out and stood beside her, still talking. The two boys had come from the barn, and they and the girls were coming up the steps.

"Head off those children," April said. "Don't let them see it."

Irene herded the children back down the steps. She sat down on the top step. Ike McCabe came out on the porch, followed by Ace.

"Send one of your boys for the sheriff," Ace said. "Leave the body where it is. Might be a good idea to put a tarp or something over it."

He turned to April, touched her gently, slipped an arm around her. She leaned heavily against him.

"The kids tipped me off," he said. "A mother doesn't

send three little girls in good shoes and clean dresses into muck like this. Not unless there's some damned unusual reason.''

Her mind was a tumble of irrelevancies. She looked into his face and was startled to see that the threat of a smile was still there at his eye corners. The memory of Carter Hanford's face strangely intruded; she saw Ace lying there instead of Hanford, dying in his own coughed blood.

"A game!" she said. "You called it a game!"

She spun away from him and grasped the porch rail. Leaning over it, she threw up into the muddy yard.

14

AN HOUR LATER, April sat at the kitchen table with Ace and the McCabes. She had drunk a cup of coffee with a touch of whiskey in it. Her stomach had settled, and she felt she could think halfway straight now.

One of the McCabe boys had been sent to Augsburg for the sheriff. At her suggestion, he had also been instructed to fetch Tom Lawrence. The other boy had gone back to chores in the barn. The girls had been sent to a bedroom. A greasy tarpaulin covered Carter Hanford's body and the bloody area around it.

"You've got title to this place now?" April asked Ike McCabe.

"Proved up this spring."

"You have a mortgage on it?"

"No, ma'am, but we might have to borrow this winter." He added pointedly, "We lost our hay...."

"What do you figure the place is worth?"

"I only got a quarter section, but most of it's good land. Leastways, it grows good hay. There's good range to the south, too, and a little piece of bottomland with wild hay that I cut. I figure two dollars an acre, at least. Then there's the buildings."

"Figure two and a *half* an acre," April said. "That's four hundred for a quarter section. Figure the buildings at six hundred. Would you say a thousand is a fair price?"

"I guess so," Ike said suspiciously.

"We don't want to sell, though," Irene McCabe said quickly.

"Well, you're going to," April said. "You're to sell to me. Let's say eleven hundred, just to be sure I'm being fair. I've had an option agreement drawn up, and I want you to sign it right now. Today."

The McCabes looked at each other in stunned silence.

"Look here, Mrs. Farnum,'" Ike said. "This is a bad thing that happened here, and you're upset. But we don't take to you telling us what we're going to do like that."

"Irene," April said, "I wanted to spare you this, but Ike is right—I'm upset. And I'm angry. I'm not going to pussyfoot. Whether you know it or not, Ike has been the cause of damage to my coaches, a whole lot of it. I'm putting a stop to it. Either he sells out to me or I'm going to send him to jail."

Ike smiled reassuringly at his wife. "That's foolishness."

"We didn't have nothing to do with Mr. Hanford coming here," Irene said. "We didn't like it. But he said—well, we couldn't go against him."

"I'm not talking about Carter Hanford," April said. "And I'm not talking about Ike sneaking around setting trip wires and things like that. Ike, do you begin to catch on? Do you see now what I can send you to jail for?"

He saw, all right, April thought. His face had turned to dough. His reply came too quickly.

"You make no sense a-tall, Mrs. Farnum."

She glanced at Ace, who was watching her closely. There was curiosity in his look and also a quiet amusement.

"It will make sense to a jury," she said. "Your fate will be in the hands of a jury, Ike. Peavey's sheriff won't be able to help you."

"Mrs. Farnum—"

"The charge will be murder," April said. "You were one of the men who killed Jim."

Ike avoided his wife's terrified look, even when she

reached out and touched his arm. He shook his head.

"That's foolishness. I never—I wasn't there."

"You were the one who pulled me into the bedroom and tied me up."

"I never. No, Mrs. Farnum! What are you trying to do to me?"

"If he was the one," Irene said indignantly, "how come you waited till now to say so? Why didn't you tell the sheriff? I don't believe you, April Farnum!"

"Jim burned your hay," April said. "Ike must have been blind mad, almost crazy. When Thorr asked him to join a party to give Jim a whipping, he jumped at the chance. I honestly can't blame him too much. Thorr is the one I would like to see punished. If I'd trusted Sheriff Haller, I'd have had Ike arrested in hope he'd name Thorr and the others who were there. But it occurred to me that Ike wouldn't be allowed to do that. He'd be reported shot while trying to escape or he'd be found hanged in his cell. Something would have happened to keep him from talking to a prosecuting attorney. That's why I didn't say anything at the time, Irene."

She paused t) let that sink in. It was true, and the McCabes knew it was true. Both of them. She could see it in their frightened faces.

"But you weren't satisfied, even with Jim dead," she went on, turning to Ike. "You still cherished a grudge. You let Thorr talk you into wrecking our stages. I've had enough of you, Ike. Sell me this place and get out of the county or go to jail—quite possibly for the rest of your life."

"You couldn't prove nothing if you tried," Ike said.

"Couldn't I? You were in Devil's Claw the night Jim was killed. A dozen people must have seen you. And a jury will believe my testimony—if Thorr and his sheriff

95

let you live long enough to face one!''

Irene exploded then. ''Damn you, April Farnum! Damn you and Thorr and Peavey & Company and your high-handed ways with people like us! Ike's a peaceable man. He got trapped between you and Thorr in your dirty stage feud. Whatever he done, he was drove to it!''

''You admit your man had my hay burned,'' Ike said righteously.

''He didn't have it burned. He did it himself. It wasn't like him. But he thought he had to hit back at Thorr some way. I don't try to justify what he did. But remember, he was your friend once. He set you up in this station. He paid for the lumber for your buildings. His men helped build the barn. When Peavey & Company came in, he let you board their teams as well as ours. You thanked him by going over to Peavey and refusing to keep our horses any longer. Yes, he burned your hay. He paid for that with his life. Even if you didn't intend to, you had a hand in his death. And you've gone on hitting at me.''

''I had to! I'm scared of Thorr.''

''Well, I've had enough of it. Now you'd better be scared of me.''

Ike glanced at Ace. ''I am, Mrs. Farnum.''

''We're caught,'' Irene McCabe said. She was sobbing, dabbing at her eyes with a handkerchief. ''We're caught between April Farnum and Jack Thorr. Good Lord, Ike, let's get out of it!''

''You're offering eleven hundred dollars?'' Ike said, his eyes fixed on the tabletop.

''Yes.''

''It's a fair price,'' Irene said. ''It'll get us off to a good start someplace else.''

''I guess so,'' Ike said. ''I guess we'll take it. We'll get out of this county. We'll get clean out of the territory.''

"This place ain't been good for us," Irene said. "We got caught in something too big for us."

"I want your word that you'll leave Montana," April said. "That's part of the deal. But there's another condition. You are to say nothing about this to anyone. You will give me an option. You will be packed and ready to clear out the moment I exercise it. One bright morning the Peavey coach is going to pull in here and find that this is my station!"

"We'll do it," Irene sobbed. The handkerchief with which she wiped her eyes was very daintily hemmed, April noticed, but it was of coarse material, probably a flour sack.

Ike got to his feet and moved behind Irene's chair and put his hands on her shoulders. Great day in the morning, April thought, he loves her. He's a miserable excuse for a human being, but he loves his wife.

She had brought an option agreement that Tom Lawrence had written that morning. Irene McCabe read it out loud to Ike, then they both signed it. April wrote a check for a hundred dollars as the option price.

When it was done, Ace, who had hardly spoken the whole time, broke his silence.

"McCabe," he asked quietly, "who killed Jim Farnum? Who struck the blow?"

Ike hesitated only momentarily. He nodded in the direction of the tarpaulin near the door.

"Carter Hanford?" Ace said.

Ike nodded again.

"Was Thorr there?"

Still another nod. "He had a bullwhip. The other man was Sid Luna. The one they call Frisco Hays was there, too, but he didn't come inside. He was the lookout."

It was almost four in the afternoon when Sheriff Haller,

Tom Lawrence and the coroner arrived together in a spring wagon. The sheriff and coroner asked their questions and made no comments. Tom Lawrence insisted that depositions be taken from the McCabes, and he made copies of each.

"You're wasting your time," the sheriff said. "Depositions aren't admissible in a murder trial."

"It wasn't murder, and there'll be no trial," Tom said. "You know that as well as I do."

"We'll see," the sheriff said.

Tom even had the two older McCabe girls sign statements to the effect that they had been hurriedly sent out of the house when April and Maidenlane were seen approaching.

Back in Augsburg that evening, April, Ace and Tom had a late supper in the hotel dining room. Pete Lafortune and Link had left for Adako Falls that morning to buy the steam engine Pete had his eye on and to make arrangements for shipping it to Devil's Claw. Link also planned to contact a banker friend in hope of making the loan they had been denied by Bart Smith.

Halfway through the meal, the sheriff arrived with a deputy and a warrant for the arrest of Asa Maidenlane. There were only half a dozen people in the dining room at that hour, but Haller made a pious little speech for their benefit. Professional gunfighters weren't going to commit murder in his county if he could help it, he said.

"You might have rich and powerful friends with enough political pull to get you off scot-free," he said loudly and with a glance at April, "but by God, I'm going to do *my* duty!"

Tom Lawrence was on his feet. He snatched up the warrant the sheriff dropped on the table. The deputy moved to a position behind Ace's chair and snatched Ace's gun from its holster.

"On your feet, Maidenlane," the sheriff said, hand on his gun butt. "Either come along now, or I'll put the cuffs on you."

The deputy prodded Ace in the ribs with the barrel of Ace's weapon. Ace stood up, giving the man a level look that backed him off.

"You'd better go along," Tom Lawrence said, folding the warrant and waving it. "There were two eyewitnesses to Hanford's death, not counting April. Both signed statements that Hanford was waiting to ambush you and that he fired at you with a shotgun before you fired. The sheriff obviously didn't bother to tell that to the judge who signed this warrant. It will be my pleasure to do so."

Ace picked up his coffee cup and drained it. With a lawman on each side of him, he marched off to jail.

"The judge boards six miles out of town," Tom Lawrence said, "but I'll see him tonight if I have to get him out of bed."

April went up to her room and found herself fidgeting, pacing the floor. Too much had happened too quickly. When she tried to read, images and anxieties raced through her mind with a frightening swiftness that shattered rational thought. She went down to the desk and ordered a tin bathtub and hot water brought to her room. After a leisurely soak, she felt halfway composed and thought she might be able to sleep. She had no more than got into bed when there was a knock on the door and she found Tom Lawrence back from his visit to the judge.

"He'll have to spend the night in jail," Tom said, "but there'll be a hearing in the morning. The judge was furious when I showed him my copies of the McCabes' depositions. He's an honest man—at least he isn't a Peavey man.

99

It's a virtual certainty that the charges will be dismissed against Maidenlane. And I daresay the sheriff will get a lecture that will leave his ears burning for a week.''

"I can see why the sheriff did this," April said. "He wants the Peavey people to see that he's doing his best for them."

"That little speech in the dining room makes it clear what he's up to. He knows he can't make a murder charge stick, but he'd like to create the impression that Maidenlane is guilty and that you have exerted some devious influence to get him off."

"Will people believe that?"

"They'll believe anything if it's presented to them in the right way. And most people don't care much for hired gun hands."

"Well, I know another honest man in this county," April said. "Charlie Moore of the *Plum County Tribune*."

Tom raised his eyebrows and quickly nodded agreement. At the time of Jim's death, the *Tribune* had published a front page editorial sharply critical of Peavey & Company's dirty approach to competition.

"I'll see that he gets copies of the depositions," Tom said.

There was the briefest of court sessions the next morning. Maidenlane was released, but he and Tom Lawrence had to stay in Augsburg a few days because the judge insisted on a continuance of the hearing. It was just a matter of technicalities, he explained. He wanted the McCabes present so the record would show their direct testimony rather than depositions. This court term was coming to an end in another ten days, and he wanted to leave no loose ends.

Meanwhile, the *Plum County Tribune* came out with a banner headline proclaiming AMBUSHER DIES IN OWN TRAP. The account of Carter Hanford's death was full and accurate. The McCabe depositions were printed in a box beside it. Readers could hardly escape the conclusion that a Peavey assassin had got exactly what he deserved.

15

THE NEW ROAD drove into the range from both east and west, a good road born in good weather and built for bad. It climbed and curled over a course chosen with an eye to gradients and drainage. It hugged the lee side of mountains, where snow would not drift. Corduroyed in gully bottoms, staunchly bridged over creeks and cuts, it stretched and squirmed to either side of the Devil's Claw crossing. Here it paused, waiting to meet itself and know the flow of life when the ferry was completed.

Pay days went by without pay for the crews. Men cursed the road, cursed Pete Lafortune, cursed April Farnum. Men who had done no work on the road showed up and cursed loudest of all—hired troublemakers, it was said, paid by Thorr.

April drew on the stage line's operating funds, on her personal account, on the ranch account. Drivers and ranch hands agreed to accept half-wages and notes for the rest. She made a small and usurious loan from a bank in Adako Falls. And at last Asa Maidenlane and Pete Lafortune rode to the work sites with a payroll. At April's insistence, the crews were paid to date plus a bonus of a day's pay as sort of an apology for the delay. Curses were replaced by plaudits. Troublemakers left, sometimes hurriedly.

Passenger traffic on Farnum stages continued to increase. Express business doubled. The figures seemed a clear indication of popular sympathy.

"We'll see how deep the feeling goes if Peavey cuts fares," April said.

"It's deeper than you think," Link assured her.

"Anyway, thanks to the mail contract, we can match any cut they make."

"Yes, but right now we need every cent we can take in."

It was early evening, and they were working together on the books. Maidenlane came through the outer office and into the room, followed by Cal, the kid from Buckley station. Cal snatched off his hat as he came through the doorway. He nodded to Link and addressed himself to April.

"Good evening, ma'am."

"Cal! Cal Buckley. It's nice to see you."

"Caulfield, ma'ma. Oc ain't my father. So it's Cal Caulfield, not Buckley."

Her smile was interrupted by a quick frown when she saw that the boy was wearing a big Colt in a tied-down holster.

"The kid wants a job in town," Maidenlane said. "I told him to talk to you."

"Cal," she said, "I need you at Buckley station. You're the one I rely on, not Oc."

"My uncle moved in with us," Cal said. "Ma's brother. He's a hard worker and he don't drink." He grinned and added, "He works Oc's tail off. Oc's scared of him."

She looked the boy over thoughtfully. The Colt had a gleam to it as if it had been recently polished. The holster had a raw, homemade look.

"Cal, where did you get that gun?"

"It's one we took off those gunslicks. I got the other, too. Ace said I might as well keep 'em."

"Why do you want to work in town?"

"I thought maybe I could work nights and when school

103

starts I could finish high school. Or I could drive stage on weekends."

"You can drive stage? A six-horse hitch?"

"I been riding to halfway station on the northbound and coming back on the southbound. The drivers have been teaching me."

"Very good. I don't need drivers right now, but I'll keep you in mind."

"I hear you'll have a steam engine to drag the ferry back and forth. Maybe I could work there."

"Maybe. I'll tell you what. Ride out to my ranch. Tell Sam Case I said you're on the payroll. He'll keep you busy till we find a permanent place for you."

"I'm much obliged, ma'am."

"And I want you to take that gun off right now. Leave it here in the office."

The boy turned to Maidenlane, who smiled gently. "She's the boss, son."

Cal drew the Colt and laid it on the table in front of April. Link slid open a drawer and put the gun into it.

"That's better," April said. "Do you realize what might happen if you ran into that pair you beat up?"

"That's why I put on the gun," Cal said.

Link swung around in his chair and hooked an elbow over its back. "That's pretty foolish. They'd gun you down and claim self-defense. That gun is an invitation."

"I can use it." Cal turned to Maidenlane for confirmation. "Can't I, Ace?"

"Fair to middling," Maidenlane said. "But Link is right. You wouldn't have a chance against either Hays or Luna."

It occurred to April that Cal would be too late for supper at the ranch, so they all went to her house, where Sally Smithwick had a roast ready. Afterward, with Cal off to the ranch and Link back to the office and his beloved bookkeeping, she and Maidenlane sat on the porch to watch the sun sink behind the Lost Tribes.

"You gave Cal that gun," she said.

"Seemed like he ought to have one."

"You taught him to use it."

"I gave him some pointers."

"Ace, that boy is sixteen years old!"

"You were right," he said. "It's dangerous for the boy to wear the gun in town."

"It's dangerous for him to wear it anywhere."

"No."

It was a soft evening scented with dust and sage. Just the smeared red rim of the sun was visible above the black mountain buttes.

"He's a good boy," April said, "but there's a fierceness in him that frightens me."

"He's a decent boy who strikes back at ugliness in the world."

"He has to learn that there are other ways to strike than with a gun," she said. "He has to."

His eyes were on her and she held his look, seeing that he related her words to himself. She tried to imagine him when he was Cal's age, another tough, decent kid striking back at ugliness.

"Cal wants to finish high school," she said.

"I intend to see that he does."

"So do I." She laughed uneasily. "We agree on something."

"Still, you don't approve of me."

She spread her hands, fumbling to frame a reply. "There's a callousness in you, Ace, a coldness that has to do with your way of life."

"My way of life," he said. "It comes between us."

105

"There's warmth in you, too, a great warmth that you don't trust. Warmth and coldness. Life and death."

The sun was gone. A single lean cloud lay above the Lost Tribes like a blade in a bloody sky. Color stained the air and touched the weathered buildings of the town with a lilac starkness.

"We became lovers," he said. "Now you put barriers between us."

She touched his fingers and his hand swallowed hers.

"No," she said. "I tear at a barrier I wish were not there."

16

ROAD AND FERRY were completed on schedule. The first stage trips over the new route were made Wednesday, September 1, 1880.

There were so many requests for tickets for the first westbound run from Devil's Claw that April ran three coaches. One was the regular mail coach that went through to Adako Falls. The other two went only as far as Augsburg and were packed with Devil's Claw residents intrigued by the novelty of making the whole round trip in a single day.

April, along with Maidenlane, Tom Lawrence and Link, rode in the first coach. Pete Lafortune rode on the box beside the driver. Tom planned to stay in Augsburg. The others would return to Devil's Claw that evening.

There was a crowd at the ferry to witness the first official crossing. There were merchants in buggies, farmers in spring wagons, kids and cowhands on horseback. Jack Thorr sat his horse well up the slope from the landing as if he hoped not to be noticed, flanked by Hays and Luna.

The ferry was a big log raft with a raised floor of heavy plank. It would carry a coach and six-horse team without unhitching, which meant it was almost a third as long as the river was wide. It was, as Pete Lafortune put it, almost as much a floating bridge as it was a ferry.

It slid between docks that Pete had built on either side of the river. On the west bank, he had blasted away most of the big rock slab that rose out of the stream. He had built a bulkhead behind this with a ramp reaching down to a floating dock. On the east bank a slip, bulwarked with logs, had been dug into the bank. There was a ramp here, too. Thus, operation would not be affected by normal changes in water level.

The steam engine was in a shed on the east bank. It was set between two winches anchored to bedrock. On the west bank, a cable ran through a huge pulley secured to the remains of the rock slab. It was a simple arrangement that could be readily adapted to horse or mule power if, for whatever reason, the engine should fail.

The trip went smoothly. Charlie Moore, editor of the *Plum County Tribune*, and other well-wishers met the coaches at the hotel in Augsburg. There was another crowd at the river crossing on the return trip and still another at the Devil's Claw office. Maidenlane proposed a champagne dinner at the hotel, but April pleaded exhaustion and went home.

There was only a dull satisfaction in having accomplished that which was universally considered impossible only a few weeks ago. She felt no jubilation, no desire to celebrate. Today's success was a victory over the river and the mountains but not over Peavey & Company. Jim's death had driven her into this fight, and she would see it through; but she was broke and in debt. And she was tired. Anger was no longer an emotion; it was a commitment, a principle, a crusade that threatened to become a way of life.

She slept late and reached the office the next morning in good spirits. She even mustered a smile for Deputy Beasely, who was waiting for her. Smug under the gleaming badge pinned to his hat, he handed her a subpoena. She had expected it, though not quite so soon, and she remarked cheerfully that it must have been brought over the new road by special messenger.

The next day she was back in Augsburg and in court,

sitting beside Tom Lawrence while Mr. Sample complained piously to the judge. While Mrs. Farnum's ferry fees for other traffic ranged from two bits to a dollar, he pointed out, she had posted the fee for stagecoaches at one hundred dollars a crossing. He requested a court ruling permitting Peavey & Company, a public carrier, to use the ferry free.

The judge brought down his gavel and said he would see counsel and Mrs. Farnum in his chambers.

"A hundred dollars a crossing," he said thoughtfully, when they were all seated. He was a freckled little man with coarse gray hair and a glary eye. "At two crossings a day, that figures out to seventy-three thousand dollars a year. That's pretty ridiculous. On the other hand, Mr. Sample, to ask me to grant your client the right to use the ferry gratis is just as ridiculous. I don't have the authority to do that and if I did, I wouldn't, and you're wasting the people's time. This is the frontier. Law is loosely interpreted and badly enforced. I'm just a self-educated country magistrate, but both of your positions are insulting to my intelligence, and I'm mad.

"The territorial legislature has the right to set tolls if it so desires. Since it didn't do so in this case, Mrs. Farnum has the right to set them. This court has no authority to interfere unless it finds that a toll is so high as to be contrary to public interest. In this case, I so find. I also find that Mrs. Farnum has every right to collect a reasonable toll from Peavey & Company. If she will, right now, in my presence, submit a revised figure, and if I consider that figure reasonable and in the public interest, I will so rule and we'll dispose of this matter without delay. Mrs. Farnum?"

April exchanged a look with Tom Lawrence. She took a deep breath and turned to Mr. Sample.

"Ten dollars a crossing, payable in advance."

"Robbery!" Mr. Sample said.

"If Peavey & Company wishes to contract for two crossings a day for a full year and to pay the entire amount in advance, the toll will be five dollars a crossing," April said. "That comes to a payment of three thousand six hundred and fifty dollars, payable before the first crossing and nonrefundable."

"Absurd," Mr. Sample said.

"Why?" the judge said sharply.

"Your honor, Mrs. Farnum is trying to gouge us. She's in financial trouble. She's trying to make a deal that will bail her out. No, Mr. Peavey will never accept."

"That's his business," the judge said. "I find the offer fair and reasonable. I see no grounds for any further action by this court. Shall we go back into the courtroom? We'll have the offer and my decision read into the record."

A few minutes later April and Tom left the courthouse together. They didn't speak until they turned down the boardwalk toward the hotel.

"You constantly surprise me," Tom said. "You might have told me what you had in mind."

"I was playing it by ear."

"No." There was a crispness in his voice that was almost an accusation. "You knew exactly what you were doing. You got exactly what you wanted."

"Not exactly. I would have liked to keep Peavey from using the ferry at all."

"Why? Now he has to do exactly what Sample said. He has to pay a fee that will bail you out."

"That's not going to happen, Tom. This is a fight to the finish, and it's not going to last that long."

That brought a frown to his face. "Don't push too hard."

"There's no sane reason for two stage lines on this route," she said. "The matter has come to a head, and it will be settled, one way or the other, very quickly. Push? For the first time I'm in a position where I can push."

"McCabe station?" he said, his frown deepening.

"McCabe station."

They reached the hotel and sank into chairs on the porch to await the arrival of the eastbound, which she was taking back to Devil's Claw. Tom had court details to attend to on this last day of the term and was staying over.

"When?" he asked.

"As soon as Peavey coaches start using the shortcut. That will be in a day or two, I should think."

When the stage pulled up, there were twelve passengers waiting to board, including April. That meant that three would have to ride on top. Disregarding protests from Tom and some of the passengers, April climbed up to the box beside the driver. In spite of the hot sun, she enjoyed every minute of the ride. When the coach rolled to a stop in front of the office in Devil's Claw, Link and Maidenlane came out to meet it. They handed her down with no show of surprise. They were becoming inured to surprise, she supposed.

"I want to talk to both of you," she said. "We have plans to make."

17

GUS PEAVEY PACED the hotel room between door and window, consuming a cigar from both ends. Mr. Sample also paced to the window, taking a tangential course and daintily avoiding collision. Jack Thorr sat tipped back in a chair with his boots on the rungs of another. Nobody except Thorr, Sample and a well-sugared hotel clerk knew that Peavey was in Augsburg. He had arrived very late the night before, had gone directly to a suite that Sample had reserved for him and hadn't left it.

It was the second day of Peavey & Company's new schedule over the shortcut. Drivers had paid toll at the ferry crossing, and everything had gone smoothly enough yesterday. But today the coach from Devil's Claw was more than an hour late. This room was directly above the hotel porch. The window overlooked the place where the coach would pull up.

"The Farnum woman should have folded up weeks ago," Gus Peavey grumbled, focusing his eyes on Sample. "You haven't been able to stop her in the courts. You haven't been able to stop her financially. What in the black damnation am I paying you for?"

"That judge is a chowderhead," Sample said. "We'll be better off without him. Court term's ended. We can make better use of the sheriff now."

"Who is also a chowderhead," Thorr said.

"Why haven't *you* stopped her?" Peavey demanded, swinging his glare in Thorr's direction. "Why haven't you burned her out?"

Thorr wished he'd kept his mouth shut. "For one thing, you said to go easy. For another, I didn't want to start a burning war with Ace Maidenlane here."

"You scared of him?"

"That bastard would burn every stack on the route. And there's something you don't know. Mrs. Farnum has got options on all the hay between here and Star City."

"What?"

"Every stem of it."

"It's true," Sample said. Peavey turned on him, and it was his turn to wish he'd kept his mouth shut.

"You let her do that?"

"Hay is not in my department," Sample protested. "I have more important matters —"

"More important!" Peavey exploded. "You know how much hay a coach horse eats during a winter? You know how many horses we stable between here and Star City?" He spat out a shred of cigar butt and turned toward the window. "Where in the black damnation is that stagecoach?"

There was a knock on the door. Sample opened it cautiously to find the hotel clerk there.

"A man at the desk wants to see Mr. Thorr. He says it's an important matter. His name is Beaumont."

Thorr got to his feet, looking grim, and left the room. Peavey moved to one side of the window so he could peer up the street. He said softly, "Sam, if anything has happened to that coach, I'm going to fire you."

Sample gasped audibly. "I have nothing to do with the coaches. I — You're joking."

"If I get mad enough to fire somebody, it won't be Thorr. If I get that mad, I'm going to need him."

Sample thought that over, trying to look amused. "If you get mad enough to give Thorr a free rein, you're going to need me, too — to keep him out of jail."

"That will take a *good* lawyer."

Sample smiled shakily. They paced in silence. The door opened and Thorr returned. He looked somberly from one to the other, cleared his throat, and spoke in a strained voice.

"That was Lenny Beaumont from Beaumont station on the old route. He says Ace Maidenlane and some Farnum people have took over McCabe station."

"*What?*"

Thorr shrugged nervously. He turned away from Peavey's glare and went back to his chair. "Lenny says Maidenlane and some kid drove eighteen of our horses down to his place this morning — all the stock we had at McCabe's. They left 'em there and made him sign a receipt. Lenny knew I was in Augsburg, and he saddled up and come looking for me. He stopped at McCabe's on the way. Maidenlane and the kid and Sam Case and Link Arbuckle was there. Farnum horses was in the barn. Link Arbuckle showed Lenny a deed to the McCabe property, signed by McCabe. He said McCabe has left the county."

Peavey dropped his cigar and ground it into the floor. Sample stood in front of the window with palms pressed against his fat cheeks.

"Lenny passed the westbound nine miles out of town," Thorr went on. "It couldn't get a change of teams at McCabe station, so it was bogged down. The worst thing is that our eastbound is due here in an hour on the new schedule. We can't send it on without a relief team at McCabe's."

Peavey's cigar was just a black spot on the floor, but he was still grinding down on it. His voice had the flat tone of an angry man straining for control.

"She won another hand."

"I'll get over to the barn and send a coach out to meet the westbound and bring in the passengers," Thorr said, getting hesitantly to his feet. "We'll have to set up a new station. Just a corral will do for the time being, but it will be day after tomorrow before the horses there will be fresh. Our schedules is shot for two days."

"There must be something you can do," Sample said. "We can't have —"

"Shut up," Peavey said.

"None of this is my department," Sample said. "But just because we're up against a bad situation —"

"What we're up against is a woman," Peavey said. He let his voice go now, and it rose till the window rattled. "A first-class, A-number-one, curly-haired, ring-tailed, she-grizzly woman! Gentleman, what we are up against is all hell boiled down to a pint."

"I got to admit it," Thorr said. "I over-underestimated her."

"You what?" Sample said.

"You're fired," Peavey said. He turned to Thorr. "And you — the lid is off. I want that station back. How deep is the sheriff in our pocket?"

"Deep enough," Thorr said.

"Good and deep," Sample said. "I saw to that."

"You're fired," Peavey said again. "Now listen carefully, Jack. I want that station within forty-eight hours. I also want that ferry. I want our people in control of it."

Thorr stared at the floor, nodding thoughtfully. "We'll have to take Ace Maidenlane out of the picture. That will be the first thing."

"Then do it. But use your head. No shooting. After that Carter Hanford mess, the newspapers would take us apart."

Thorr scowled. "I'll figure out some kind of an accident."

"A nice clean accident," Peavey said.

115

18

The Farnum westbound was late.

Maidenlane lounged on the steps of McCabe station and watched Cal move the relief team, rigged and ready, to the side of the barn so it would be out of the sun. Sam Case and Link Arbuckle stood together just inside the arch of the barn doorway, consulting their watches every minute or so.

Maidenlane had asked Sam for two men from the ranch to help move Peavey horses out and to man the station temporarily. Sam had come himself and brought the kid. Link had brought McCabe's money and a deed to sign. The four had seen the McCabe family on its way and would stay until the Stone family, who had operated the old Farnum station a mile east, moved in here and took over.

The kid came around the barn, glanced anxiously down the road and walked toward Link and Sam. Maidenlane got up and joined them. Link had his watch in his hand again.

"Twenty minutes now," he said. "Not enough yet to worry about."

"Just the same, I'll saddle up and have a look," Maidenlane said.

"I'll ride along," Cal said.

"No, thanks." The kid looked disappointed and Maidenlane added, "My job, son. Yours is here."

He threw his saddle on a big gray he had taken a liking to. As he led it out of the barn, the coach pulled up. The others hurried to meet it. There were only five horses in the hitch.

"Ambushed!" the driver shouted from the box. He handed the reins down to Sam and climbed down. The coach doors opened and passengers spilled into the yard.

"We was on a little upgrade," the driver went on, "and we was moving at a walk. There was just one shot, and the off point horse dropped dead. Shot came from a patch of woods about a hundred yards to the right."

"You were at a walk?" Maidenlane said.

"That's what makes no sense. The bloody bushwhacker could have spilled the coach if he'd picked a place where we was traveling faster."

"You see anybody?"

"Nothing. I didn't go poking into those woods."

"Seems like the feller didn't want to hurt anybody," Sam Case said. "Either that or he didn't know his business."

"He knew his business," the driver said. He touched a finger to his temple. "Bullet caught the horse through the top corner of the blinder close to the cheek strap. Animal was dead that instant. It was a jim-slicker of a shot."

"How long ago?" Maidenlane said.

"About an hour."

Passengers were clustered around, looking grim. Maidenlane made his way through them and mounted the gray. As he rode out of the yard he touched his hat to Cal, who was among the coach horses, unsnapping tugs. The boy touched his hat in the same way.

He found the dead horse beside the road at the place the driver had described. He rode on slowly, scanning the ground beside the road for a sign. A stone's throw down the slope he found it — the shoe marks of a saddle horse that had angled away from the road toward a stand of timber on a small rise to the north.

The plainness of the trail was almost like insolence. He followed it to the trees and into them to a tiny open place. There was a ragged rock formation here and a stand of grass around it. The ambusher had dismounted here and walked back to the edge of the woods. Tracks were indistinct in the pine duff, and Maidenlane left his own horse and scouted on foot.

It was easy enough to find the place where the man had waited for the coach. He had scuffed around as if he had waited impatiently. He had then shot a walking horse a hundred yards away cleanly through the blinder. Being in no immediate danger of pursuit, he could readily have shot another — or for that matter, all six. But he had not. And the one he had chosen had been a point horse, one of the pair that would damage the team's efficiency the least.

It wasn't like Thorr to make gestures, Maidenlane thought as he returned to his horse. Too late, he realized he might have ridden into a trap. He positioned the reins and was reaching for the stirrup when Frisco Hays stepped from behind the rock formation. Hays was looking over the barrel of a rifle aimed at Maidenlane's head.

Maidenlane stepped slowly away from the horse, raising his hands. From somewhere behind him came the voice of Sid Luna.

"Just stand easy." Luna moved close and snatched the revolver from Maidenlane's holster.

"Hallelujah," Hays said. "Our enemy hath been delivered into our hands."

"The boss was right," Luna said. "He came alone."

"It is not good that man should be alone."

"Get the horses," Luna said. "I got him covered."

Hays went off into the pines and returned riding one horse and leading another. He covered Maidenlane with a revolver while Luna mounted. They filed out of the woods

118

and took the road eastward. Hays took the lead. Luna, gun in hand, brought up the rear.

The road dipped into a little ravine, climbed a hogback and swung north along the rim of the Devil's Claw gorge. Hays looked down at the river below.

"We leadeth you beside the not-so-still waters," he said, half-turned in the saddle.

"Shut up," Luna said.

"Why not right here?"

"Keep going."

"Yea, let us ride upon the high places of the earth."

Maidenlane began to understand. They meant to throw him over the edge. Hays grinned at him.

"Vengeance is mine, saith the Lord."

"Vengeance?" Maidenlane said. "I could have finished you boys off at Finchleen station."

"That crazy kid damn near did. You delivered us unto our enemy."

"And Carter Hanford was a friend of ours," Luna said.

"Therefore shall thy calamity come suddenly," Hays said.

Maidenlane glanced back at Luna. "What's the matter with him? He swallow a Bible?"

"His daddy was a preacher. Turn around and shut up."

They rode in silence for a time. When the road bent abruptly away from the gorge, they no longer followed it but continued along the rim. The ground became rocky and uneven. Occasionally there were shale-filled pockets that they had to circumvent. The river wound below like a silver ribbon. They were perhaps two miles south of the ferry crossing, Maidenlane guessed.

"This is far enough," Luna said.

They halted. The drop here was about two hundred feet, Maidenlane estimated. A man who went over the edge would be as certainly dead as if he caught a bullet between the eyes. His body would be swept downstream to be snagged on rocks somewhere in the gorge — or perhaps to be washed ashore in the vicinity of Devil's Claw town.

"Step down," Luna said.

Maidenlane ran his glance over the ground ahead. Fifty yards away there was a depression, a steep-sided little pocket. It extended to the cliff edge so that it had the shape of a bowl with a piece broken out of it.

Just below this pocket the cliff wall bulged a bit. Irregularities in it formed a crude human face in profile. The rim was rounded to form the forehead. A shelf of projecting rock was the nose. A juniper grew out of the shelf with a tuft of foliage at its top that from this angle looked like low-set eyebrows. Below the nose-shelf was a niche and another shelf so that the face seemed to be that of a man with his mouth open. A man screaming, Maidenlane thought.

"Step down," Luna said again. "Or had you rather have a bullet in your gut?"

There was something revealing in his tone—a touch of bluff that shouldn't have been there. He won't shoot, Maidenlane thought. By God, they're under orders not to shoot except as a last resort. They were going to knock him cold and throw him off, and it was supposed to look like an accident. No bullet in the body when it was found. Probably they were going to force his horse off the rim, too. No bullet in the horse either. It would look as if the horse had lost its footing and plunged into the gorge with its rider. At least no one could ever prove otherwise.

That was all a guess. But it was all there was, and he acted on it.

He dismounted slowly. Then he ducked swiftly under

the head of his horse and reached for Hays, dragging him from the saddle, throwing a clublike blow at his head, landing solidly. Both horses shied and galloped off. As Maidenlane reached for Hays's gun, Hays's horse bumped him and sent him staggering before he could grasp it.

Luna plunged toward him, leaning from the saddle and chopping with his revolver. Maidenlane glimpsed the blow coming and tried to dodge. It knocked his hat off and caught him at the base of the neck in a staggering burst of pain.

Luna wheeled his horse and spurred forward for another try. Maidenlane dodged again, making a grab for the gun hand and missing. There was something wrong with his left arm. He could move it but there was a great weight in it and a cumbersome numbness.

Hays was on his feet, holding a gun and coming toward him. Luna leaped from the saddle. Maidenlane ran, moving away from the cliff. They raced after him, Luna yelling to halt or he'd shoot. Maidenlane bore southward toward the two horses that had shied off and were grazing a stone's throw away. When the two men moved to cut him off, he turned and raced for Luna's horse.

He reached it a few steps ahead of them, but there was no time to catch up the reins and mount. He slapped it on the rump and choused it off toward the others. That made it a foot race, a deadly game of tag among men who wore boots and were saddle stiff and not limber on their feet.

He was faster than either of them, but he was running north — away from the horses. Luna was cursing, yelling threats. As Maidenlane put a little distance between them, one of them fired a shot over his head. There was reassurance in that. Either of them could have dropped him easily enough if they hadn't been under strict orders not to do it that way.

121

They broke off the chase and ran back toward the horses. They would ride him down. He raced for the bowl-like pocket ahead. He reached its edge a few seconds after Hays and Luna reached the horses. They were coming on at a lope.

He plunged down the bank to a barren floor freckled with rock outcroppings. He threw himself behind one of these and lay flat, breathing hard. Peering around the end of the outcropping, cheek against the ground, he watched as they reined up at the edge of the pocket. They rode a short distance to their left, where the descent was less abrupt, and guided their horses down to the floor of the pocket.

They hadn't spotted him, but they knew he was here. Beginning at the west side, they rode slowly toward him, zigzagging among the rocks. A hundred feet away, Luna saw him and fired, not trying to hit him, ricocheting the bullet off the rock. Maidenlane rolled to his feet and darted to another outcrop closer to the rim of the gorge, then to another. He had some wild hope of keeping out of sight until he could surprise one of them, drag him from the saddle, get his gun. But they dismounted now and came toward him cautiously.

He was trapped against the rim. He looked over it and saw the top of a juniper below him. Below it, he could see just the tip of a ledge that it grew out of. He remembered the face he had seen in the cliff. He was directly above it.

He moved closer. The top of the scraggly tree was a good twenty feet below him. The surface of the cliff above it was a sixty-degree slant of solid rock, but it was slightly rounded — the forehead of the grotesque face. He remembered that there was a niche below the ledge and another ledge below that — the open mouth of the screaming face.

Hays and Luna were sixty feet away, staying close together, sure of him now. There's no good thinking about it, he told himself. It's a better chance than fighting two men who will eventually shoot me if they can't beat me any other way.

He picked up a loose rock and hurled it at them. They dodged easily, Hays laughing aloud. Luna fired a shot that spattered against rock a yard to Maidenlane's right. Maidenlane took a step backward. Pretending to slip, he sank to his knees and pushed himself over the cliff edge.

Belly against the steeply sloping rock, arms spread and pressing hard to slow his descent, he slid painfully down to the juniper. He clutched prickly foliage, felt the little tree bend. Its meager, rock-entwined roots held. It lowered him to the first ledge. He let it swing out again, dropping him lower. There was indeed a sizable niche in the cliff, and a second ledge. Luck was with him. He landed solidly and rolled into the niche.

He lay panting, his injured shoulder throbbing. He heard Hays's and Luna's voices above him. Only a word now and then was clear.

"...gone to glory."

"Can't see anything down there...river swallowed him..."

"Rejoice, thine enemy falleth."

They were looking down on the upper ledge. They couldn't see that there was another below it. They could only conclude that he was dead and gone forever.

He eased himself onto his back and waited. After several minutes he saw them against the skyline to the south. They were trying to maneuver his horse over the edge. The gray resisted in panic as they backed it close. Then a hind foot slipped and they pushed the animal over. Gutsick, Maidenlane watched it somersault stiffly on the long fall to the river.

He waited a time before he moved. Hays and Luna might very well linger in the vicinity, sweeping out tracks. When he judged that it was safe, he stood up, rubbing his bad arm, flexing it, testing his grip. Mincing along the ledge, he made a dismal appraisal of his situation.

The upper ledge was nine or ten feet above this one; he could see no way to get up there. And above that was twenty feet or more of smooth, unclimbable rock. Looking northward, he traced the river to a bend half a mile upstream. The ferry crossing was somewhere beyond that, hidden by twists and lurches in the narrow canyon. There was no way he could signal it. No one would come looking for him until he had been missing at least overnight. If Hays and Luna had swept out tracks, there would be nothing to bring searchers to this off-trail place on the canyon rim — ever. Every hope he could muster seemed unlikely.

The shelf he was on was partly a recess in the cliff, partly a projecting stratum of rock. To the south, it disappeared entirely. Northward, it dwindled down to a ledge a foot or two in width; then it widened a bit and continued, sloping downward very gradually. Sometimes it broke off for short distances; but when it did, there were other irregularities in the wall that looked as if they might offer a foothold. A climber might work his way along it for a considerable distance. Maidenlane could see no way up or down from it, but surely there were ledges and toeholds that he couldn't see from a distance.

He began to pick his way along the ledge, quickly realizing how tedious and how exhausting progress was going to be. He was not a practiced climber. He had to learn as he went along, and he moved with wormlike slowness, checking and double-checking the way ahead, rehearsing each move in his mind before he made it.

For hours he clung and crawled, inching horizontally across the cliff face, finding no way up or down. With night seeping into the canyon, he reached a projecting point and made his way around it. Surprisingly, there was a tiny, blind side canyon behind the point. Its walls were crumbling. It was full of debris and its floor rose sharply from the level of the river.

Fifty feet away and a little below him there was a place where the wall was crumbling away. Over the ages, bit by bit, shale had flaked off and built up into a towering pile, a steep half-cone of loose rock against the cliff. If he could work his way to the top of it, it would be a way down to the canyon floor.

Fifty feet. There was no projecting stratum here that offered a marked route. Darkness was closing fast. Immediately in front of him a rounded face of rock bulged out of the cliff. He pulled himself upward along its curve, reached its top, and rested. Exhausted beyond the physical, he fought a dazed reluctance to go on. Shakily, he stood on the slippery rock, found hand and toeholds, and climbed to a little protrusion with dwarfed brush growing on it. Beyond this there was a slash in the cliff face, a long, shallow niche that he could crawl along.

He reached the end of it and was above the cone of crumbled shale. But he had moved upward as well as horizontally; he was thirty feet above it. He could see no way to climb down to it. All that was left was one last long chance. He swung his feet off the edge and jumped.

19

HE WOKE LONG enough to know that he was in a bed. Across the room a lamp burned softly under a red and blue shade. There was a great pain in his left leg when he tried to move. Then there was warm, sweet oblivion again.

There was a doctor peering over low-riding spectacles, and sporadic consciousness while he probed the injured leg. He spoke of the Achilles tendon and the peroneus tertius. Working up, he mentioned the peroneus longus, the gastrocnemius, and the semimembranous. The semimembranous was a mess, he said.

"Strained ligaments, maybe some broken cartilage," he said. "No broken bones, and that's a wonder, but he can't walk. Don't let him try."

Then there was daylight in the room. There was a woman beside the bed and there was the feeling of a long-ago time. She smoothed his hair. He looked into her face and saw beyond the hardness and the makeup and the years.

"Dolly."

"Well, he knows me this morning."

"What day is it?"

"Friday."

"It ought to be Wednesday."

He scowled at the ceiling, trying to remember. He had jumped. He had hit the pile of shale, his left leg plunging into it deeper than he had intended. He somersaulted, sharp rocks tearing at him. He plummeted downward in an avalanche that would bury him. . . . He couldn't walk. He crawled across the ragged floor of the little canyon to the

iver and filled his belly with water. . . . How long had he
een in the canyon before the log came down the river?
One night, maybe two. He had matches in his pocket and
e had built a fire. . . . The log slid along slowly, close to
hore. It had been left over, no doubt, from the ferry-
uilding. He crawled to the river and slithered into it and
aught the log. He got aboard it and rode it down the
orge. Lying prone on it, he lapsed into sick and shivering
emiconsciousness, knowing nothing except that he must
ling to the log. . . .

A sudden fear stirred in him, and he made an effort to
et out of bed. Pain tore him. Dolly gently held him down.

"Thorr," he said.

"Rest easy, lover. Jack don't know you're here."

"He thinks I'm dead?"

"Everybody thinks you're dead. They found your
orse yesterday."

He tried again to get out of bed and couldn't make it.
His whole body was a sodden weight. The slightest effort
o move his leg brought tooth-grinding pain.

"Nobody knows you're here except me and Doc and
he girls," Dolly said. "And Andrew. Andrew found
ou."

He stared at the ceiling, remembering the rest of it. He
was clinging to the log and there was a bridge. There was
a man on the bridge, poking him with a fishpole. He
rabbed the pole. The man walked along the bridge,
owing the log to shore. . . . He leaned on the man, half-
arried by him, and they got to a buggy. He pulled himself
nto the buggy, getting tangled in fishline and a tie-line
astened to a sash weight. . . .

"My being here is a risk for you," he said. "There are
ther places I could go."

"No risk, lover. Jack doesn't want people to know he's in this business. He never comes here. Besides, I owe you."

"Owe me?"

"Do you think I don't remember how you looked after me when Dad died? He left me with a slow-minded brother and a tent saloon at the end of track. I was sixteen years old."

"And redheaded and freckled. And pretty."

"And a fool," she said. "You made a deputy's pay. The U.P. paid Jack four times that much, not counting the graft. I was flattered when he wanted me. You tried to stop me from going to him. He tried to kill you. I owe you for that."

"He had other reasons to kill me."

"He ambushed you and left you for dead. Now it looks like it's happened again."

"Help me out of bed," he said. "I want to see if I can stand."

"Not yet, lover, not for a while. You've got to lie there and hope everything slips into place and heals straight. You're lucky. You've got a whole house full of nurses."

'em, and I'd just as soon blow you to hell as not. Give him the deed.''

"Yes, sir." The sheriff tried to smile and didn't make it. He reached slowly around to his hip pocket and got the deed. Sam Case took it and shoved it into his boot. Cal backed off toward the doorway.

"Get back inside, kid," Sam said. "And get rid of that gun."

Cal lowered the Winchester, pointing it at the porch floor. He held it in one hand with his finger still on the trigger.

"Drop it," the sheriff ordered. "Walk over to the rail and drop it into the yard."

"Do as he says," Link said.

Cal stepped to the porch rail, reaching over it but hesitating to drop a cocked and loaded rifle. Frisco Hays was standing in the yard below him and a little behind him near the end of the porch. Sid Luna was at the other end of the porch near the steps. Hays seemed startled by the appearance of the rifle above him; he lunged toward the corner of the porch as if to take cover behind it. He took just one step, clutching at his revolver but not drawing it. Luna peeled his gun from its holster and fired twice, fanning the hammer. Cal staggered into Link's arms, gave the world a look of bewilderment and collapsed.

Link sank to the floor with the boy, tearing at the bloody shirt, seeing two bullet holes high in the boy's chest. People milled close, laying words on the air. Link answered, his words unreal. He heard the sheriff's voice.

"...fool kid threw down on Deputy Hays. Deputy Luna fired. It was his duty."

Link got to his feet, hazily picking out Hays and Luna among the many people on the porch. They were both wearing deputy's badges.

21

SHERIFF HALLER, FOLLOWED by Hays and Luna, entered the Peavey & Company office in Devil's Claw town. The front window had been broken, and the clerk was sweeping shattered glass into a dustpan. The man who had replaced Carter Hanford as office guard stood nearby, a shotgun in the crook of his arm. He nodded at the sheriff and waved him toward Thorr's office.

Thorr was at his desk, eating a sandwich and drinking a glass of buttermilk. Hays and Luna dropped into chairs. The sheriff worked up his smile and jerked a thumb toward the outer office.

"Vandalism?"

"The whole county is mad at us," Thorr said. He wiped his mouth on his sleeve. "You boys shouldn't have shot that kid."

The sheriff shot a glance at Luna. "It was unavoidable. The kid —"

"Sure," Thorr said. "The way you tell it, he asked for it. But he was a kid, and folks is mad as hornets. You'll never win another election, and old Gus is going to have to fire me as soon as this shivaree is over. It don't matter. The Farnum woman will be out of business. Folks will have to ride Peavey coaches or stay home. We got just this one more thing to do."

"When?"

"Tonight." Thorr picked up the glass of buttermilk, scowled at it and set it down without drinking. "You and your boys will show up at the ferry. You will rule it unsafe and you will take possession of it in the public interest."

"I'm finished in this county," the sheriff said. "I'll be

lucky if the county board lets me serve out my term."

"Like I said, I'm finished, too."

"Gus will sugar you off good. What about me?"

"You been on the payroll. You got to earn your money now, that's all."

"I've been earning it and you know it. If I take over that ferry, it's going to cost you real money."

"There'll be a bonus for you if everything goes smooth."

"I want five hundred dollars, Jack. Half now."

Thorr finished the last crust of his sandwich. He scowled at the buttermilk again and took a sip. "Five hundred, then. You get it tomorrow morning when the ferry is in your possession."

"You got some more boys for me?"

"Your deputy got 'em. He lined up some drifters, three of 'em."

"Beasely? You talked this over with him?"

"Bud and me has been working together a long time."

Frowning, the sheriff nodded his acceptance. "I'll look up Beasely and deputize the new men."

He left the office. Thorr stared grimly at the unfinished glass of buttermilk. Frisco Hays broke the silence.

"Money maketh many friends."

"If word of this leaks out, that Farnum woman won't sit back and do nothing," Thorr said. "She'll have her people fort up at the ferry and try to stand off the law."

"Our lips are silent and our tongues are still," Hays said.

"You got it wrong," Thorr said. "I want her forted up."

"That means shooting," Luna said.

"You boys make damn sure it means shooting. Now listen careful. When the sheriff's party gets close to the

133

landing, you leave and circle into those hills behind it. Then you fire. On the sheriff. It will look like the first shots come from the Farnum people.''

Luna grinned appreciatively. ''Even Haller won't know the difference.''

''He won't know nothing. He'll be dead.'' Thorr waited for that to sink in. ''Make sure of it. Take a buffalo gun.''

''That'll leave Beasely in charge,'' Luna said.

''He'll be easy to handle. It will be you boys who is in charge.''

There was a silence. Then Luna asked uneasily, ''You'll be here?''

''I got to go to Star City. That's what you say if anybody asks.'' Thorr gave a little twist of his head. ''I ain't going to make it, boys. It come on me strong when Carter Hanford was killed, but I fought it off. It come on again after you boys put Ace Maidenlane away. I been going through hell.''

He found a scrap of paper, scribbled on it, folded it, and gave it to Luna. ''Take that over to Dolly right away.''

22

APRIL FARNUM HAD never been inside the Star Bucket before. She pressed through swinging doors and paused to look over the afternoon customers. There was a moment of suspended animation. Men stood frozen at the bar, staring. The barkeep stood with his arms spread along the bar as if to hold it down. The faro dealer halted with fingers on the box and didn't deal.

Sheriff Haller stood behind the seated faro players. Deputy Bud Beasely was beside him. April aimed herself at the sheriff. He took off his hat and smiled.

"If you want to talk to me, Mrs. Farnum, we'll go down to the deputy's office."

"There's a rumor that you have plans to take possession of my ferry," April said.

"Shall we talk privately?" The sheriff put on his hat and reached for her elbow in an effort to turn her back toward the doorway. She shrugged out of his grip.

"Is it true?"

"Ma'am, there's been a misunderstanding. I intend to inspect your ferry, that's all."

"Inspect it for what?"

"Safety, ma'am."

"You crossed on it this morning, didn't you?"

"Yes, ma'am."

"Was it safe?"

"I didn't inspect it."

There was laughter in the room and a jeer or two.

"Is it true that you intend to take half a dozen armed deputies along on this inspection trip?"

"Ma'am, I have a duty to the citizens of this county. I

owe it to them to make sure that ferry is safe."

"Yesterday you took over McCabe station, even though I have a deed to it. A sixteen-year-old boy was killed. Did you owe that to the citizens of this county?"

"That boy had a gun, Mrs. Farnum. He was taking aim on Deputy Hays."

"Three members of the Stone family were eyewitnesses to what happened. They say you're a liar."

There was a low swell of voices in the saloon. It was closer to a murmur than a cheer. But it was sympathetic and encouraging, and April's confidence surged. They were with her, all of them. She could make them cheer if she tried.

"All right, Mr. Haller," she said. "You may inspect my ferry. You and one deputy. Men from my ranch will be on guard. If you approach within one hundred yards with a party of armed riffraff, deputized or not, we will stop you."

The sheriff looked around the room, which was silent now, awaiting his response. He pushed his hat to the back of his head. "Mrs. Farnum, are you saying before a room full of witnesses that you will fire on my men?"

"On Thorr's men, Mr. Haller. Everyone in this room knows that Peavey & Company owns you and that your intention is to declare the ferry unsafe and take possession of it and see that it is operated for the benefit of Peavey & Company. I'm not going to let that happen."

"Whatever you think of me, ma'am, I'm duly elected sheriff of this county and I'll do my duty as I see it."

"You murder children," April said.

She turned on her heel and marched for the door. A man she knew slightly stepped away from the bar as she passed. He was perhaps slightly drunk. He had a glass in one hand and he snatched off his hat with the other.

"If you need more men at that ferry, Mrs. Farnum, I'm volunteering."

A man seated at a table shot to his feet. "Me, too, Mrs. Farnum."

"Thank you very much," she said. She reached the doorway and turned. "I—I'll let you know."

She turned up the street and walked the two blocks to the Farnum barn. Abe Klingerman saw her coming and came into the yard to meet her.

"Abe, do you have a horse handy that will carry sidesaddle?"

"No—Well, I got one in the back pasture. It'll take a few minutes to catch her."

A few minutes probably meant twenty, she thought, knowing Abe. She marched into the tunnel of the barn and led him past stalls of coachers to the back, where three saddle horses were stabled. She pointed to a big chestnut gelding.

"Put a sidesaddle on this one."

She was in no mood to ride astride today—not in the rather trim, ankle-length skirt she was wearing. It and her petticoat would bunch up around her hips. With the whole town watching, there she'd be, trotting off in her long, frilly bloomers.

"He ain't broke to sidesaddle," Abe protested.

"Then I'll break him."

"Ma'am—"

"Please, Abe. I'm in a hurry."

She rode the gelding around the barnyard a few times before setting out. The strange saddle made him nervous and a little balky, but he didn't try to throw her. She reined into the street, rode at a trot until she was out of town and then urged the horse into a canter. Insecure under the unfamiliar distribution of weight, he wove from side to

137

side occasionally, but he gave her no real trouble.

In an hour she reached the landing. Link, Pete Lafortune and Sam Case were there, along with the two men who operated the ferry and half a dozen ranch hands. They were all armed to the teeth.

Sam Case caught the reins of her horse. Link came up to give her a hand down from the saddle.

"You can do no good here, ma'am," Sam Case said.

"I tried to tell her that," Link said. "It was like talking to a gatepost."

She gave them a quick smile and got down to business. "I want you to mark a place on the road a hundred yards from here. Put up a pole with a rag tied to it, something like that. I told the sheriff we'll fire on his party if more than two men come closer than that."

"You talked to the sheriff?" Link said.

"You bet I did."

"We're not bluffing? We'll fire on the law?"

"You're dad-slapped right we will," Sam Case said. "The law! A smiling hypocrite with grab-shooter deputies!"

"Sam," April said sternly. "We're here to save this ferry, not to settle scores. I want you to forget about Cal."

"Forget!"

"Do you think I don't know how you feel? Do you think I'll ever be free of the screaming guilt of that boy's senseless death? But tonight we're putting it out of our minds. We'll fire if we must, but we'll fire the first shots over their heads."

"If they fire back?"

"I told the sheriff he'll be allowed to approach with one deputy. I hope that's what he'll do. I pray it is. But if he tries to take the landing by force, we'll fight."

"I picked these men careful," Sam said. "There ain't a

married man here, and they're all willing to do the necessary."

Most of the men were standing within earshot. One took it upon himself to speak up.

"We say hooray, ma'am."

"Only thing is, you shouldn't be here, Mrs. Farnum," another said.

"Of course I should," April said.

A chuckwagon had been brought from the ranch. A cook and helper produced a meal of beans, bacon, biscuits. It was served on tin plates and everyone washed his own.

There was a long, five-foot-high woodpile in front of the engine shed. Some of the men took positions here. Others took cover on the ferry itself, which was in its slip. At sundown a lookout galloped up and reported that the sheriff and a party of six men were on their way.

Link took April into the engine shed and behind one of the big windlasses. "Promise me you'll stay here. Please."

"If there's shooting, I'll get behind something and stay there. Meanwhile I intend to see what's going on."

Link walked up the road to the pole that had been planted to mark off a hundred yards. The sun still shone on the hilltops; but here in the pocket of the landing it had dipped behind the mountain wall, and he was a lonely figure in the twilight. He was a man with no taste for violence, April thought; yet if it came, he would face it as steadily and as competently as he did everything else.

Five riders came into sight at the top of the slope above him and began the descent down the curving road. Sam Case and Pete Lafortune watched from in front of the engine shed, standing close to the woodpile and looking over it. April joined them, calling to the lookout who had brought word of the sheriff's approach.

"There are only five riders," she said. "You said there were seven."

"There were when they left the other road," the man replied. "Two must be hanging back for some reason."

"Or circling," Pete Lafortune said. "They might have some idea of getting behind us."

He had field glasses and he scanned the high country to the east through them. Then he swung them to the hills behind the landing to the north.

"May I have them?" April said, holding out her hand for the glasses. She focused them on the approaching riders and picked out Sheriff Haller and Bud Beasely, who was easily recognizable with his badge pinned to his hat. She didn't recognize the other three riders.

"Were Hays and Luna with them when you saw them?" she asked the lookout.

"Yes, ma'am, they were."

"They're not there now."

"Pass the word," Pete said. "Two men may be up there in the hills behind us."

"I'll take a man and find some cover tother side of the engine shed," Sam Case said. "Protect our rear."

Link waited at the hundred-yard marker. As the sheriff's party approached, he stepped to the middle of the road. He raised his hands in a gesture that meant stop and that also showed he was unarmed. The sheriff reined up. The other riders halted in a ragged front behind him.

April watched tensely. Link gestured, pointed toward the landing. He was telling Haller what she had told him in town: he could approach with one deputy, no more. Surely, when Haller saw that her crew was ready to fight, he would agree. Or he would call the whole thing off. Surely he had a little sense left....

140

Suddenly, senselessly, shots shattered the silence—a single booming report followed by a rattling fire that echoed across the little gulch. They came from the hills behind the landing. At first, April assumed her men were being fired on; then she saw that the sheriff had fallen from the saddle. Link and one of the deputies bent over him. Other riders threw themselves from their horses and ran, crouching, to the cover of rocks or brush.

"Get down!"

Pete's arm was around her, pulling her down behind the woodpile. The sheriff's men were firing now—at the landing. A bullet spattered bark from the woodpile above her head. A ricochet screamed behind her.

"Don't shoot!" she screamed at her men. "It's a mistake! They think we fired on them." To Pete, she said, "Wave a white flag. We have to explain."

"Too late."

Shots came from the other side of the engine shed now, close at hand. Sam Case had spotted the men to the north and was firing on them. There were answering shots from that direction. There was a clang from the engine shed as a bullet struck metal there.

April found a gap in the piled wood that she could peek through. Up the road, horses were scattered on the hillside while their riders fired from cover. Link, too, had taken cover.

"That's Hays and Luna behind us," she said. "They shot the sheriff. It was deliberate."

"Yes," Pete said. "That first shot sounded different from the others. Louder. A Sharps .50, something like that. A buffalo gun that would be accurate at the distance. The other man opened up with a Winchester to add to the confusion."

April's men, with the exception of Sam and the man

with him behind the engine shed, did not fire. After a moment or so, firing from up the road tapered off to an occasional shot or two. Shooting at the rear stopped altogether. Sam Case came around the engine shed, running in a crouch. He sank down beside Pete and April.

"I got those two behind us spotted. I propose to take two men and go up there and get 'em."

"They'll pick you off before you get to the foot of the hill," Pete said.

"No, sir! I got a route figured where they won't see us till we get there."

"Might be worth a try." Pete looked at April.

"I'll go along with Sam's judgment," she said.

"I ought to be the one to go," Pete said. "Not Sam."

"You think I'm too old?" Sam snorted.

Pete grinned. "It will be a hard climb."

"At a nickel a puff, I could get rich racing lard-butt engineers uphill! Anyhow, I've studied out the lay of the land, and I'm going."

He picked two men and led them down to the river, where they could move under cover of the bank to a patch of pine at the foot of the hills. They could be glimpsed from time to time as they picked their way through the trees and up a steep hillside, concealed from Hays and Luna by the curve of the slope.

April peered through the woodpile in the other direction. Link was up there, obviously a prisoner. Heaven knew what abuse he was taking. Bud Beasely would be in charge now. Why didn't he send Link down with terms or demands or whatever?

One of the men behind the woodpile fitted his hat on a slab of wood and raised it. It immediately drew a bullet.

"They sure mean business," he said, examining the hole in the slab. "This feller got it right in the nose."

23

"SAM'S COMING BACK!"

A man near the end of the woodpile was pointing northward. April moved so she could see around the engine shed. Sam had come out of the trees near the foot of the hill. He was alone. He didn't bother about cover from the rear, but as he crossed the ravine he was careful to keep the engine shed between him and the men up the road. He reached the shed and covered the few feet to the woodpile in a sort of running dive.

"They moved out," he announced. He delved into a pocket and produced a cartridge casing as big around as a man's thumb and as long as his middle finger. "Found this."

"Fifty caliber," Pete said.

"I left our men up there," Sam said. "We're protected from that direction now."

"Are two men enough?" April said.

"Got 'em forted up at the tippy-top of the hill. They could hold off an army."

One of April's men called out that something was happening up the road. April peeked through the hole in the woodpile and saw a man coming toward them, holding his hands high. Darkness was seeping into the ravine, but she could still recognize him easily enough. It was Link.

Pete stood up, waving a white handkerchief above the woodpile. April rose beside him. Link walked straight up to the woodpile and halted about six feet in front of it.

"I've got orders to stop here," he said. "There are three guns aimed at my back. Beasely says you are all to come out into the open with your hands up or I'll be shot."

"My God," Pete said, the words barely audible.

"Beasely said that?" April said. "A law officer would have you shot in cold blood?"

"Hays and Luna are there now. They're telling Bud what to do."

"They were back there behind us," April said. "One of them shot the sheriff."

"It was clear enough to me where those first shots came from," Link said. "But Beasely and the others won't admit it. They insist you fired on them."

"Thorr wanted the sheriff dead," Sam said. "Beasely must be in on it."

"*Is* the sheriff dead?" April asked.

"He was still alive when I last saw him," Link said, "but just barely. The slug almost took his arm off. They tied him on a horse and took him back to town. My guess is he bled to death on the way."

Sam pulled a slab of wood off the pile and let it drop at his feet. He did the same with another. He was standing directly in front of Link.

Beasely called down from the slope, his voice thin and high-pitched but the words crisp in the quiet dusk.

"One minute! They surrender or we cut you down!"

"They've got us," Pete muttered.

"No," Sam said. He pulled another slab off the pile. Pete caught on and he, too, began dropping wood on the ground.

"Pretend we're talking real serious," Sam said to Link. "Ease up closer. Slow. An inch at a time."

In a moment there was a dip in the woodpile that was a bit less than waist high.

"That's enough," Link said. "I can make it."

"Everybody down when I say go," Sam said.

"There are three guns aimed at him," April said. "He can't—"

"Yes, ma'am," Sam said. "We got to have some kind of distraction-like, something to make those gunnies glance away from their sights for just a second. Do something to make 'em look at you, ma'am, and then duck fast."

She was already stepping out of her skirt and petticoat. She had a curious impulse to strip off everything, to step out in front of the enemy stark naked. She walked past the end of the woodpile in her frilly, below-the-knee bloomers. She held her petticoat in both hands and waved it.

"Go!" Sam said.

She darted back behind the woodpile and crouched. Link took a long, rolling dive over the low place in the pile. Everybody else ducked.

Shots rattled across the little valley too late. Link was unscratched. Firing was heavy for a few minutes. Sitting on the ground, April struggled into her clothing. She was embarrassed now, and the thought occurred to her that she may have laid another legend on the West. The men here would tell of her performance as long as they lived. With, no doubt, variations.

The shooting stopped. Darkness thickened. She could no longer see the pole that marked the hundred-yard point up the road. There was a rosy haze up there, though, the glow from a fire built behind cover. Beasely's men seemed to be settled down for the night.

"They'll let no Farnum stage pass in the morning," Link said. "We ought to get word to our drivers to go back to the old route and the old schedule."

"Peavey coaches will have to go back to it, too," April said.

"Unless Beasely gets control here. Seems like he'll have to make a move tonight."

"No chance of that," Sam said. "We'll post guards. All he can do is sit up there and block the road."

"Beasely's over his head," Link said. "Hays and Luna are calling the tune."

"Which means Thorr is," April said.

"From what I heard up there, he's gone to Star City."

"That seems peculiar."

"Maybe not. He can claim he was out of town and knew nothing of any of this—if we ever get to court."

"We'll get to court," April said. "Tom Lawrence is on his way to Helena to try to get a special court session to deal with the McCabe station business. This outrage will give him new grounds. But even if he fails, even if I go broke, I promise you I'll face Gus Peavey in court . . . ."

She finished weakly, suddenly unsure of herself. Sheriff Haller was very likely dead. Thorr would claim that the sheriff alone was responsible for the McCabe station matter and for this attack on the landing, too. Moreover, Beasely and his men would swear that the sheriff was killed by a shot from the landing. In court, it might all look pretty bad.

The people of the county had sided with her, April thought. That was the one thing in her favor. She remembered the men in the saloon who had volunteered their help. She came to a sudden decision.

"I'm getting an idea," she announced. "I'm going back to town. I'm going to tell what has happened here. And I think I see a way to get our coach past Beasely in the morning."

Link regarded her doubtfully.

"Suppose thirty or forty people from town come out here in the morning," she went on. "Unarmed people.

Suppose they just simply swarm all over Beasely and his crew and insist that the stage go through.''

"By God," Sam Case said. "It'll work."

"I don't know," Link said. "I don't see how she can raise that many people."

"She can raise a hundred! Folks are ready to help if somebody shows 'em what to do."

"I'll have to sneak out of here the back way," April said.

"Climb that hill behind us and work your way cross-country," Sam said. "Sooner or later you'll hit the road."

Link thought that Sam should go with her, but she insisted that he was needed here. Every man would be needed if Beasely tried an approach during the night. In the end, it was decided that Sam would go to the top of the hill with her to make sure the men posted there didn't mistake her for the enemy.

They went on foot across the ravine and up the slope, leading April's horse. It was good and dark now, with only a faded fragment of moon hanging above the horizon to the east. Sam signaled the men on the hilltop with a series of owl hoots, and the pair came to meet them. They boosted April into her sidesaddle.

"Just point your horse at the moon," Sam said.

It was not so easy as that, of course—not in mountain country without even a trail to follow. At the bottom of the hill she found herself in a sharp gully. Her horse, still fretful about the sidesaddle, wanted to turn right. That was the short, sensible way to town, but it would have led back toward Beasely's camp. She reined left and as they climbed out of the gully they were headed away from the moon. Moreover, a slope to the east was too steep to climb; she had to continue north and west. She reached a summit and was above the gorge. That was frustrating, but at least there was a long downslope ahead of her that she could work across in an easterly direction.

The horse was snorting loudly. She pulled up to give him a breather, but he didn't want it. He was plainly out of patience with a rider who had worked into the mountains in the wrong direction, and he wanted to get to town and the solace of a barn as quickly as possible. She sensed that he would welcome the slightest excuse to get rid of her. But when it came, she was immersed in her own impatience and unready for it.

She never really saw the night-hunting creature that provided it—just a pair of gleaming eyes in a patch of brush to her right. A bobcat probably. The horse shied and broke into a run. When she tried to rein him in, he put his head down and bucked. She fell backward over the saddle and out of it. She lost her hold on the reins and found herself rolling to her knees and screaming at a horse that galloped away pointed at the moon.

She was unhurt. She trudged after the horse, telling herself that he wouldn't go far with dragging reins but not really believing it, not of this horse. Suddenly she came upon a wagon trace. It undoubtedly led to the north-south stage road, she thought. It was a way back to town, and that tickle-brained horse would know it and wouldn't stop till he was in Abe Klingerman's barn.

There was a small ranch in the foothills here somewhere. She supposed that the wagon trace might take her to it. But the trace puzzled her. In the other direction it slanted up toward the gorge. She wondered who used it and why.

Then she saw a hazy square of light above her in that direction. There was a cabin up there, perched on the shoulder of a mountain. Someone was there. Surely there would also be a horse she could borrow.

It was a tiring climb. She reached the top and paused a moment for breath. She was on a sort of shelf, with the cabin backed up against a big rock outcroping. A shadow crossed the lighted window, then another. As she approached the door, she heard voices inside—a man's, a woman's. She knocked on the door.

24

ALONG ABOUT THE middle of the morning the black woman came to his room with a pitcher of hot water. Previously, she had shaved him and given him a sponge bath in bed; now he limped to the washstand and did for himself. She brought breakfast, and he sat down to eat it at a small table by the window with a view of the barn and chickencoop and Andrew gathering eggs. Beulah and Andrew were the only ones in this house who got up much before noon.

"I was to the store," Beulah said as she straightened the bed. "There's talk about a hooraw down to McCabe station. The sheriff and some deputies took it away from the Farnum people."

"Took it away?" Maidenlane said. "Mrs. Farnum had a deed."

"There was shooting. A boy was killed."

Maidenlane watched her smooth the bedclothes. He put down his fork. "What boy, Beulah?"

"I don't know. Folks is all stirred up about it."

"A boy. You hear his name?"

"No, sir. The sheriff turned the station over to Peavey & Company. They own him, folks say. They say he ought to be run off."

"The sheriff shot the boy?"

"I think it was a deputy."

"I want you to find out about that boy. His name. Who shot him. Will you do that for me?"

"When I can get away. This afternoon."

"What happened to my boots?"

"Doctor cut them off you, Mr. Maidenlane. I took

them to the bootmaker. Miss Dolly told me to. He's making you a new pair the same size. You ain't ready for boots yet, though.''

''Was that boy's name Cal?''

''I don't know,'' Beulah said.

Dolly showed up in the early afternoon with dinner on a tray. This was the heavy meal of the day. There was ham, mashed potatoes and gravy, green peas, biscuits. She sat across the table from him and ate with him. He pressed her for news, but she knew no more than Beulah had told him.

''I'm going to be gone for a while,'' she announced. ''Two-three days.''

''Where?''

''All you have to do is sit tight and get fat. Beulah will look after you.''

''Where, Dolly?''

''None of your business, lover.''

''You're going somewhere with Thorr.''

''You afraid I'll tell him you're alive?''

''No, not that.''

''Then mind your own business. Beulah said you asked about your boots. I was going to surprise you with a new pair. They'll be ready by the time you need them.''

''I can walk. I've got to get out of here, Dolly.''

''You can barely hobble, lover. Relax. Get fat.''

Later he sat by the window and watched Andrew bring the horse out of the barn, hitch it to the buggy and drive around toward the front of the house. He had no view of the street, but he heard the front door slam and knew Dolly was gone.

He limped to the door of his room and called into the hall for Beulah. She came up the back stairs wearing a small straw hat with a red flower in it.

''You find out about the boy?'' he demanded.

"I'm on my way out now."

"Where's Dolly gone?"

"I was told you'd ask. I ain't going to say."

"Where are you going?"

"To the store. It's the best place for news."

"Stop by that bootmaker's. If the new boots aren't ready, bring me a pair of good-enoughs."

She seemed about to protest, then she gave him one short nod and went back down the stairs. He limped to his table and sat down with a pack of cards. He played solitaire for a while, getting up occasionally to test his leg. It pained when he put his weight on it. He had a feeling that it was likely to collapse under him at any moment.

He tried to concentrate on the cards and not think about the dead boy. He watched Andrew return and unhitch the buggy. He heard the front door and supposed Beulah was back, but she did not come upstairs at once. He was lighting a lamp when she finally showed up.

She was carrying a tray with poached eggs and toast and a coffee pot on it, and she had a market basket hooked over her arm. She set the tray on the table.

"The boy's name was Cal Caulfield," she said.

Maidenlane stared at the poached eggs. Beulah poured coffee into his cup.

"I guess you knew him."

"I knew him."

"I'm sorry, Mr. Maidenlane."

"He was one of the rare ones, Beulah. The world has a way of killing them young."

Beulah sat down on the bed. "It was Sid Luna who shot him. They say the boy had a gun. Luna was wearing a badge."

She was still holding the market basket. She took a pair of boots from it and held them up. "These are your old ones. Bootmaker didn't have no good-enoughs to fit you. He sewed up the left one where the doctor cut it.''

"Give them to me." He kicked off carpet slippers and pulled on the boots. There was still swelling in his left leg, and the boot went on painfully.

"There's more news," Beulah said. "Eat something while I tell it to you."

"Tell it."

"The sheriff come to town today. Mrs. Farnum walked into the Star Bucket and gave him a tongue lashing. Now him and a bunch of deputies have gone out to take away her ferry. But she's got a bunch of her ranch hands out there. She rode out there hell-to-split on a sidesaddle and a horse that ain't broke to it.''

Maidenlane gulped down the last of his coffee. He took a few tentative steps in the boots.

"I can't stop you from leaving," Beulah said. "Maybe you ought to set down and think, though. That leg ain't going to hold up."

"I'll stop by the doctor's place, have him bind it up. Where's Dolly gone?"

"That's got nothing to do with you."

"If she's with Thorr, it has."

"The truth is I don't know exactly. A cabin someplace. He's on a drunk. He beats her, Mr. Maidenlane."

"Andrew will know where," he said.

He limped to the closet, where he took his gunbelt from a hook and buckled it on, holster empty. As he turned to face Beulah, he stumbled and nearly fell. He hobbled to the table and sat down.

"That's right," Beulah said. "You ought to stop and think before you try something you ain't up to."

"Tell Andrew to hitch the buggy," he said.

Twenty minutes later he was beside Andrew in the buggy as it pulled up in front of the doctor's house. Half a dozen men were standing in the yard in lantern light. As Maidenlane eased down from the buggy, they crowded around him, shining the lantern in his face. There were soft and profane exclamations of astonishment that he was alive.

One of the men was Abe Klingerman. "The sheriff's inside," he said. "He's shot up — dying maybe. One of his ragtag deputies brought him in and then cut out in a hurry."

Maidenlane climbed the steps and went into the house. The sheriff was on a bed in the room the doctor used for an office. He was covered with blankets up to his neck. The doctor's wife held a cup to his lips, urging him to drink.

The doctor gave Maidenlane a look of surprise over his glasses. Then he jerked his head toward the sheriff.

"Big slug shattered the humerus just below the tuberosities. Tore up the deltoid muscle and the pectoralis major. Nicked the artery and he would have bled to death, but he had the presence of mind to wad up his hat and tuck it into his armpit to shut off the flow of blood. If we can keep him from going into shock, he's got a chance, I guess. He'll lose the arm, though."

The doctor's wife stepped away from the bed. The sheriff stared at Maidenlane.

"You?"

"It's me. You think you were in hell?"

"Am I dying?"

"Maybe not. Doc hasn't made up his mind."

"Luna shot me," Haller said weakly. "The bastard had a buffalo gun. He and Hays — left the party. Thorr must have — ordered it."

154

"You hear that, Doctor?" Maidenlane said. "It might be important."

"Clearly."

"Look here, Sheriff," Maidenlane said suddenly. "I want a badge. Deputize me."

Haller stared vacantly; then a sly appreciation crept into his expression. "By authority — vested in me — Hell, you're deputized. Take my badge."

The doctor's wife pointed to a table where Haller's handgun, badge, and other possessions lay. The gun was a .44. The cartridges in Maidenlane's belt would fit it, and he shoved it into his holster. He picked up the badge. There was a smear of dried blood on it like pink lacquer. He pinned it to his shirt without wiping it off.

He sat down and shucked out of boots and pants. He put his left foot on a chair and the doctor wrapped his leg tightly and ingeniously, grumbling that he guaranteed nothing.

Abe and the men in the yard had been joined by others. They saw the badge on Maidenlane's shirt and were full of questions and helped him into the buggy.

He and Andrew drove north along the dark stage road in silence. They reached the junction with the road to the ferry, but Andrew drove past without turning.

"Whoa!" Maidenlane said. "Where you going, Andy?"

"Dolly," Andrew said.

"Not yet. Turn around."

"He beats her up."

"First, the ferry. Then we'll go get Dolly."

Andrew took a moment to respond. Then, with obvious reluctance, he swung the buggy off the road and began a wide turn. As he did so, they heard the soft hoofbeats of a horse coming down the road from the north.

"Whoa! Pull up," Maidenlane said.

The horse materialized out of the darkness, traveling at an easy canter, reins flying, headed straight for town. It was riderless but carried a saddle. A sidesaddle.

25

SO FAR, IT wasn't so bad, Dolly thought. Jack had made
love to her right off, before he'd had more than a couple of
pulls at the bottle. Now he was pouring it down heavily,
but he was in a talking mood. He was bragging that he had
the Farnum woman beaten now. He had dealt with Ace,
and now he had beaten her, and he was king of the hill. He
kept repeating himself and was sometimes hardly cohe-
rent, but Dolly pretended to listen with great interest.

"Handsome woman," he said. "Smart. But I done her
in. You kill the county law officer, you're done in."

Dolly supposed he was just babbling, but it was important to keep him talking. "What county law officer?" she
said.

He was sitting at the table in his underwear. Looking
pleased with himself, he got up and found his watch and
made a little show of looking at it. He came back and sat
down again and took a long pull at the bottle.

"Haller is dead by now. The Farnum people killed
him."

Dolly wondered if he was making sense or just dream-
ing out loud. She reached for the bottle and held it to her
lips, pretending to drink deeply. Thorr laughed. He liked
to see her drink.

He drank and talked on. Sometimes he giggled like an
idiot. That was bad. When he reached the giggling stage,
he was unpredictable, dangerous. Dolly praised him,
agreed with him, laughed with him — anything to keep
him talking. Suddenly he reached across the table and
slapped her.

She tried to get to her feet, but he pushed the table into

157

her. She tripped over her chair and fell. He poured whisky on her, giggling. She pretended to want a drink, and he gave her the bottle. There was about an inch and a half of whisky left, and he insisted that she drink it all. He watched closely, and she had to do it. She got up, gagging, and went to the sink, where there was a bucket of spring water. He followed her, snatching a fresh bottle from the shelf by the stove.

There was a sharp knock at the door. They both froze, looking at each other in disbelief. Thorr put down the bottle and looked around for his gun. There was another knock. Dolly went to the door and swung it open.

"Please," April Farnum said. "My horse threw me. Could I ——"

Thorr flung the door wide, knocking Dolly aside. He seized April by an arm and yanked her into the cabin. She made a gasping sound, got her balance and freed herself from his grip. She ran her eyes over his underwear-clad figure and then looked him in the eye.

"Mr. Thorr."

He stared back at her. He giggled uncertainly. She turned and addressed herself to Dolly.

"My horse threw me. I must get to town. May I borrow the horse I saw outside? I'll have him returned to you the first thing in the morning."

"Sure," Dolly said desperately. "I'll help you saddle him."

Thorr leaped between them and the door. He swung backhanded at Dolly, who stepped backward and avoided the blow. He placed his hands on April's shoulders and marched her backward, pressing her into a chair beside the table. She seemed to understand that she was up against a maniac and she made no effort to resist. She even managed a small smile.

"I shan't intrude on your — party, Mr. Thorr. If I can just have that horse, I'll be on my way."

"You sit tight," he said.

He backed away from her toward the bed, keeping his eyes on her. He bent and reached under the bed, revealing a triangle of bare rump where a button on the flap of his long johns was missing. He dragged his shoulder holster from under the bed, removed his short, heavy revolver from it and flung the holster aside. He came back to the table. There was a drawer in the end of the table. He opened it and put the gun into it.

He sat down at the end of the table behind the drawer. Dolly was puzzled as to what he was up to, but she sensed a sly purpose behind the action. She stepped close to him and spoke urgently into his ear. Sometimes if she did that, she could make him listen.

"Jack, her horse threw her. People might come looking for her. For God's sake, get her out of here."

He pushed her aside. He beamed smugly at April.

"Handsome woman. Smart."

He touched her cheek. She moved away from his hand but with no show of distaste. She adjusted her chair so it faced the table. She seemed simply to be making herself comfortable. Dolly had to admire her control.

"Mr. Thorr," April said. "Aren't you going to offer me a drink?"

He extended the bottle, but she didn't take it.

"Could I have a glass, please?"

Thorr regarded her with a steady amusement. He got slowly to his feet. The drawer in the table was open about an inch. He backed away from the table, watching April closely.

He was deliberately challenging her, Dolly realized. She was his enemy. She was probably capable of killing

159

him if she got the chance. He knew that. He wanted her to make a try for the gun. He wanted her hatred to explode in order to trigger his own.

She seemed ready to take the bait. Her eyes flicked to the drawer, measuring her chances. Dolly snatched up a tin cup and plunked it on the table. She picked up the bottle and poured a small drink.

"Sorry," she said. "No glasses."

April touched the cup to her lips, saying cheerfully, "Here's to all of us." Thorr came back to the table and took a drink from the bottle. She tried to stand, but he reached out and kept her in her chair.

"I got you," he said. "I beat you and now I got you."

He giggled.

Dolly went to the door and pulled it open. She met Thorr's eyes and said, "I'm sick. I got to go."

She stepped into the darkness, closing the door behind her. Thorr's bridle hung on a nail beside the door. She took it and headed for the picketed horse. There was no time for a saddle. If April Farnum could somehow get to the horse, she would have to ride bareback.

The door flew open and Thorr came after her, waving the revolver. He snatched the bridle from her and struck her with it, herding her back to the cabin. April tried to move around them as they came inside, but he spun her around and marched her back to her chair.

"Such hospitality!" she said.

He giggled. He put the gun back into the drawer and sat down, leaving the drawer open. He began to press her a bit more boldly, touching her arm, her neck, her breasts. She pushed his hand away and told him smilingly to mind his manners. Again, Dolly had to admire her composure. But it wouldn't save her. The demon had him. He would prod her till she showed hostility. Then God help her. And me, too, Dolly thought. He won't want a witness left alive.

He reached over the table with both hands, his belly pushing against the drawer and closing it. He took April's head in his hands. His fingers touched hairpins and he pulled them out, tumbling her hair to her shoulders.

"Hallelujah," she said calmly.

He studied the hairpins with drunken fascination. He made a fist and inserted them between his knuckles with their sharp points protruding.

A small motion at the window caught Dolly's eye. She glimpsed a face there. She asked herself if her mind was playing tricks, but she knew it wasn't. It was just a glimpse, but the face was Maidenlane's.

He could shoot through the window, she thought. Then she realized that he couldn't; from that angle April was squarely in front of Thorr. The door. If she could open it . . . She found herself on her feet.

"I'm going to open the door and get some air in here."

It was a mistake. As she reached for the latch, the door flew open. Maidenlane lunged into the cabin, gun in hand. He turned quickly to avoid bumping into her and his leg gave way. He fell, dropping his gun hand to the floor to catch himself.

Thorr sprang to his feet, upending the table and pushing it in front of him as he charged. It crashed into Maidenlane, knocked him flat, fell on top of him. Thorr ran around it and yanked out the drawer upside down. His revolver fell out and he snatched it up. He flung the table aside and held the gun to Maidenlane's head.

Maidenlane's gun was on the floor beside him. Thorr kicked it away and picked it up. April bent over Maidenlane, saying, "Ace, Ace . . ." over and over again. With her help, he got to his feet. Thorr stood with a gun in each hand, looking from one to the other. Jubilation crept into

161

his face. He seemed about to giggle, but he did not.

"You ain't dead," he said. "So I will do it after-all."

He was sobered, Dolly thought. But the demon would quickly return.

"You're wearing a badge," Thorr said.

"The sheriff didn't die," Maidenlane said.

Thorr weighed that, staring at the badge. "He's dead. How else would you get it?"

"He gave it to me. He's talking his head off, Jack."

Thorr gestured with his left-hand gun. "Get down to the end of the cabin. Down there by the bed. Both of you."

They obeyed slowly, Maidenlane limping.

"Set down on the bed."

The whisky bottle was on the floor, its contents spilled except for a few ounces. Thorr gestured to Dolly to pick it up. He tucked his left-hand gun under his right arm, took the bottle and drank.

"Get down there with them," he said to Dolly.

The others were seated on the bed. She stopped near them, staying on her feet. Thorr fired a shot into the floor in front of her.

"Set down."

She obeyed. Thorr backed to the sink, put down the bottle and reached under the sink for the kerosene can. He came toward them, giggling, pouring kerosene on the floor.

Maidenlane stood up. "For God's sake, Jack. Let the women go. This is between you and me."

Thorr fired into the floor again, inches from Maidenlane's toes. "Set down!"

Maidenlane sat. Thorr came closer, giggling, pouring kerosene.

"Jack," Dolly said desperately, "I want a drink. Let's

162

open a new bottle. Let's all have a drink."

He lunged close, dousing her with kerosene. He lunged again, dousing the others and quickly retreating. He backed toward the door, splashing the floor, the walls, the upset table. When the can was empty, he opened the door and flung it into the darkness. He reached around the jamb and got the open padlock that had been left in the staple there. He held it up for them to see.

Maidenlane sat tensely on the edge of the bed. Dolly watched him out of the corner of her eye. He was braced for one last hopeless rush, she thought. With his bad leg, he had no chance at all. I'll rush, too, she thought. It will be better to be shot than burned alive.

Strangely, Maidenlane gave an emphatic nod of his head, then another. She looked past Thorr and saw the figure in the doorway with hands raised above his head and a questioning look in his eyes. She, too, nodded.

Andrew brought down his weapon with all his strength — the twelve-pound sash weight that was used as a tie iron.

They stood outside the cabin, breathing deeply of the night air. Andrew finished saddling Thorr's horse and brought him up.

"Nothing seems real," April said. "I couldn't believe it was happening. Now I can't believe it's over."

"Over," Dolly said. "Over, over, over."

"Not yet," Maidenlane said. He took the reins from Andrew.

"You can't ride!" Dolly said. "Not with that leg. Let Andrew take the horse."

He made the quick and painful effort and was in the saddle.

"Ace!" April said. "Where — ?"

"The landing," he said.

"No! Listen to me. Wait! I have a plan. The people are angry. They want to help...."

He had swung the horse away and was on the road down the mountain.

26

HE DID not try to deny the pain but only to detach himself from it. He thought of it as a substance, a thing as external as the misshapen moon or the darkness or the twisting trail. It mattered only insofar as it might slow him or work to the advantage of the men he would meet ahead in the night. The meeting was his duty and his destiny; he doubted that not at all. There would be more death at the meeting, theirs or his or both. That, too, he accepted with detachment.

He reached the north-south road and urged the horse into a lope, bracing himself with his left hand on the fork of the saddle. When he turned into the new road and the horse slowed on the upgrade, he withdrew his left foot from the stirrup for what little relief that brought.

When he judged he was about a quarter mile from Beasely's camp, he halted and slid from the saddle. Looping reins around saddlehorn, he pointed the horse toward town and slapped it on the rump. He left the road and moved parallel to it, hobbling, staying behind cover when he could.

He sighted the picket just beyond a bend in the road, a tall man with a slouch to his shoulders and a rifle tucked under his arm. Maidenlane worked his way across a slope and crept close, keeping low, staying in the shadows of rocks and brush. The man stood in the road, not moving much. This was a south slope and rocky; he kept watching the ground as if wary of night-hunting rattlers. When Maidenlane saw his chance, he stepped up behind the man, whipped the rifle from the crook of his arm and flung it away.

The man whirled, startled almost out of his wits, groping vainly for the rifle. He found himself facing Maidenlane's revolver and raised his hands.

"Unhitch your gunbelt and drop it. Use your left hand."

The man obeyed. His eyes took in the badge on Maidenlane's shirt. "Who the hell are you?"

"Let's say I'm the acting sheriff. How many other pickets has Beasely got out?"

"One. At the east end of the ravine the other side of camp."

"What's your name?"

"Davis."

"You lie to me, Davis, I'll kill you. You understand that?"

"Why would I lie? This ain't my war."

"Just passing through?"

"That's right. I was offered twenty dollars to pin on a badge and help the sheriff do his duty. Didn't know what I was buying into." Davis added, "Guess the sheriff didn't either."

"Where are Hays and Luna?"

"Bedded down."

"How many others in camp?"

"Beasely, one other."

Maidenlane gestured with the gun. "Walk ahead of me. Slow and quiet."

The camp was over the crest and to the right of the road, a ring of gear around the smoldering remnants of a fire. Men lay inside the ring with feet toward the fire, four sleepers evenly spaced like spokes in a wheel. Maidenlane softly ordered Davis to halt.

"Lie down on your back," he whispered. "Head toward the fire. Don't make a sound, don't move, and you'll live another day.''

Maidenlane eased into the camp. He studied the sleeping figures and identified Beasely, Hays, Luna. All were wrapped in blankets. Weapons were close at hand.

He stole close to Beasely and moved a rifle and revolver out of reach. As he turned toward the man on Beasely's right, his bad leg failed him and he almost fell. He stood motionless for a moment, breathing deeply. Then he silently moved away a rifle that lay beside the sleeper, a man he didn't know. There was a gunbelt, too, and he slid the revolver from its holster. With a gun in each hand, he positioned himself between Beasely and the unknown man. Hays and Luna lay beyond the frosted ashes of the fire, Luna slightly to the left, Hays to the right.

Hays slept with his head on his saddle. His gunbelt was looped over the horn and a rifle lay beside him. Another rifle, a long buffalo gun, was propped against a rock near Luna, but his handgun was not in sight. He slept with it under his blanket, Maidenlane concluded.

He pointed his right-hand gun in the air and fired. As he expected, Luna flung off his blanket and came up with a revolver in his hand. Maidenlane fired both guns into him and, thumbing back hammers, swung them on Hays, who was reaching for the holstered gun beside his head. He had it clear when Maidenlane again pulled both triggers.

The man to the right was on his feet. Beasely was groping around for weapons that weren't there.

"Stand easy and you won't get hurt," Maidenlane said, not looking directly at either of them. He limped past the fire, turned Luna over and saw that he was not breathing. Hays was on his back. He looked up emptily, his lips moving.

"Amen," he said and died.

27

THEY GATHERED on the main street before dawn — tradesmen, close-in ranchers, ranch hands — everyone that the word had reached, women and children with them. They came on horseback and in buggies and buckboards and farm wagons. There were more than a hundred of them and they left town at first light with the Farnum coach in the middle of the procession. They carried no arms. They meant merely to parade through Beasely and his men and see the coach on the ferry and on its way to Augsburg.

As it turned out, they needn't have bothered. Half a mile along the new road they met Deputy Beasely coming in. There were three riders with him and two horses with dead men slung over the saddles.

Beasely would have led his men through the procession without a word; but April, who was riding in a spring wagon beside Abe Klingerman, stopped him and demanded to know what had happened.

"Maidenlane," he said.

There was a tear in his hat where he usually wore his badge. His holster and saddle boot were empty. So were those of the others in his party.

"He took one of our pickets in the dark. He disarmed him and came into camp." Beasely nodded at the corpses. "Luna reached for a gun. I guess Hays did, too."

He moved on. So did the column of citizens. April tried to think coherently. She had won the war with Peavey & Company. There would be work now, lots of hard work. There would be decent, businesslike solutions to problems. Gus Peavey might very well offer to meet the pric

168

she had quoted him. If he did, she would up it another five thousand. At least five thousand, she promised herself.

The people broke into a cheer when they came in sight of the ferry. The hundred-yard pole was still standing. April told Abe to pull off the road there, and they watched as the others rattled and galloped down the slope. Her crew was gathered around the chuckwagon for breakfast. She picked out Ace and Link, sitting together with plates on laps. They saw her and waved. When Link saw that she was not coming down, he borrowed a horse and rode up the slope.

"Is Ace all right?" she asked, as he reined up beside the wagon.

"I don't know how he did it," Link said. "He can hardly stand."

"Take him to the ranch. See that he has everything he needs."

Link regarded her strangely. "Sure."

"Be sure the doctor sees him."

"Sure."

People swarmed over the landing. The coach rolled down the ramp onto the ferry. Wheelblocks were dragged into place, the cable tightened, and the craft eased out of its slip into the stream. A dozen kids went along for a free ride.

"We need men like Ace," Link said. "The world needs them."

"Unfortunately," she said.

Link looked at her strangely again. Ace looked up from his breakfast and waved at them. If she went down there, she thought, she would take him into her arms in front of everybody. That would amount to a declaration, a commitment she was not yet ready to make.

Her war was over. Was his? She wouldn't ask him that,

but he would ask himself as he must have asked a hundred times before. The answer had always been negative but now at least he would ask again.

''Turn around,'' she said to Abe. ''Take me back to town.''

Below, Ace put his plate aside and got unsteadily to his feet, watching as the wagon circled.

His answer would be perceptive and honest, and she would trust it.